I0547830

Alternative Measures:

A Novella

By

Sonny Girard

Sonny Girard

ISBN:0982169639
ISBN-13:9780982169636

This work is dedicated to my mother:

Sorry you missed too much of the good stuff

R.I.P.

- With love, your son

PROLOGUE

SOUTH PHILADELPHIA STREET – Near future – 7:15 p.m.

Pouring rain adds to the darkness and desolation in this area of warehouses, factories, and stores that are shut down tightly by this time. Large droplets from the charcoal sky splatter and explode off black enamel fire-escapes to reflect a glitter from street lamps, and off ominous-looking cement gargoyles at the tops of doorways. Rain pounds swelling pools of water like little explosions.

In the middle of the block, a warm yellow light glows through the miserable night from the *Pinar del Rio* restaurant. Inside, a birthday party is in progress for four-year-old Maria Santiago. The warm party atmosphere, full of color, bright lights, and celebratory Latin sounds is a stark contrast to the bleakness outside. The room is decorated with pink and white balloons and matching streamers offset by the red, blue, and yellow colors of Colombia. Scents of garlic, cilantro, cumin, and paprika permeate the air. Cigar smoke swirls to the ceiling. *Aguardiente* and rum colas are poured non-stop. The music is loud, rhythmic, and contagious, as evidenced by all the bodies in motion; whether dancing, swaying, or merely finger-tapping. Even in the chaste celebration of a child's birthday, sex exudes from women undulating to the music in too tight or too short dresses; seductive breasts threatening to escape from the low cleavage cuts of colorful fabric. One woman holds her dress up near her hips as she gyrates to the drumbeat of the music. Old men ogle her and smile

1

appreciatively as they remember a time when they could have made use of her charms. An infant sleeps through it all in a bassinet.

Outside, a dark blue van pulls up a few doors away from the *Pinar del Rio* restaurant. The side door slides open and two men in dark slickers and heavy boots jump from the van into puddles of water. They slosh off toward the party.

Maria's father, Juan, and the restaurant's chef, enter through the swinging kitchen doors and carry an oversized birthday cake to the center of the room and set it on a table. It is decorated with figurines of children's cartoon characters Dora the Explorer and Diego. Juan ignites five tall sparkler candles on his daughter's cake with a solid gold lighter. The Latin music stops and Happy Birthday singing begins. Maria sticks her finger into the side of the cake to steal some whipped cream.

The two men in slickers reach the restaurant's door. They swing it open to let the bright light flood out onto the street. The sudden light makes them squint even as they smile at the partiers who have turned to greet more guests. Instantly, the new arrivals lift their slickers to expose two Ingram MAC-11 machine pistols and begin to fire into the room.

Bursts of blood and bone fly as bullets tear through the partygoers. A waiter is pinned upright against a wall as machine gun fire keeps his dead body from falling. Screams and wails combine with the cacophony of gunfire to a dizzying assault on the ears of whoever has caught safety on the floor behind a piece of furniture or under a warm corpse. Acrid smoke from the guns and exposed intestinal material would be nauseating to anyone still alive not too panic-filled to notice. Bullets easily cut through the cake's yellow sponge and fudge cream into Juan Santiago and his wife, throwing them backwards over chairs and onto the floor. A .380 ACP round pierces five year old Maria Santiago's eyeball and opens a gaping hole in the back of her skull, ending not only the party at hand but all her future birthday celebrations.

An alarm clock rings incessantly on the nightstand closest to Nicole Gianetti, who views the 6:15 through a web of tangled eyelashes and dry sleep. She throws an arm over her ear and across her chin-length hair dyed sandy blonde from its natural Mediterranean near-black.

"Shit…already?" she mutters to herself.

Nicole reaches for the snooze alarm with her eyes shut and after fumbling over the clock presses the button. Awake, but reluctant to start the day, she snuggles deeper into her bedding and rubs herself with the sensuality that a lover would. The sensations of her fingers manipulating her tender flesh lead her into a daydream where a faceless male softly kisses her neck, her breasts, her stomach, while her fingertips gently trace that path on her living skin. As the imaginary lips brush her between her legs her fingertips touch wetness and slip inside her; their motion in and around the sensitive area bring her to the beginning of what should lift her on a wave of sexual release.

The alarm rings again: 6:30.

Nicole refuses to leave her delicious fantasy, while moving her fingers more quickly. They begin to irritate her moist entry as much as the incessant ringing does her ears.

"Alright, alright," she snaps, while shutting the alarm and dragging herself from the bed. Her frustration turns her grumpy as she crosses the room decorated as brightly as a prison cell: black and gray shades of furniture and accessories straight out of Conran's; simplicity to a point of bareness. She stumbles against a black dresser with no religious or other decorative items, save one photo of an elderly couple against a Florida background of greenery and one close up of a fortyish, clean-cut, successful-looking man.

Edgy from having her daydream interrupted, Nicole throws a gray flannel robe on, pulls it tightly shut, and shuffles off to a tiny kitchen where she microwaves a cup of coffee that has already been prepared the night before and stored in her refrigerator for the early morning. The sound of steam begins to hiss from the radiator.

"It's about time."

Nicole looks at a Chinese takeout restaurant calendar, which shows it is Valentine's Day. Beneath the calendar, on the kitchen counter, is one Valentine's Day card, with a title that reads, "To a Wonderful Daughter on Valentine's Day." The solitary card throws her deeper into this morning's funk. Adding moody to edgy, she sips her coffee then shuffles off to the bathroom.

In the shower, Nicole tries again to lose herself in her romantic vision with the previously faceless male who, with some difficulty on her part, has become that of the photo on her dresser. Her breathing becomes quicker and shallower as she struggles to build toward a climax. Her body feels ready to swell, ready to take her on a ride over waves of ecstasy…but she loses it as slides away quicker than it was climbed.

Angry and unfulfilled, Nicole dresses, grabs her briefcase, and goes to her front door, which she opens to find her daily newspaper outside. When she lifts it and turns it over, she reads the headline: "SLAUGHTER AT WEST SIDE BIRTHDAY PARTY."

"Fuck!"

2

"Fuck," Mayor Jonathon White, a tough blue collar-type in a white collar suit and tie, says, as he reads the same headline as Nicole Gianetti, but focuses more on the subheading: "MAYOR DROPS IN POLLS – PARTY CONSIDERS NEW CANDIDATE FOR GOV'S RACE." He shakes his head at the photo of the *Pinar del Rio* slaughter site, in which he stands. Crime Scene Identification Technicians scour the carnage for shreds of evidence; the walls are torn up from gunfire, blood is everywhere, and chalk marks and triangulated string identify where bodies fell. The Mayor tosses the paper onto the floor without regard of whether he's screwing up a piece of vital evidence.

District Attorney Edward Marshall, whose face is in the photo on Nicole's counter, stands alongside the Mayor. "When you called and told me you had been here all night, I figured no one would have had the guts to show it to you," he says.

"Or too much consideration...something my District Attorney has never been accused of."

D.A. Marshall just shrugs.

Mayor White gestures toward the open front door, where a crowd of reporters strain against a police cordon; many of them hold umbrellas to protect against the continuing rain. "How come there's never a shortage of reporters, Edward?" he asks. "No matter how short we run of everyone else, they keep multiplying."

"More blood attracts more sharks."

"And we have certainly been bleeding lately. Come on, Edward; let's go out the back way."

"Don't you want to throw them a piece of chum?" the D.A. asks. He checks a call coming in on his phone and ignores it.

"I already gave them a statement before you got here. Besides, it doesn't matter what I say," Mayor White continues. "Their stories are all pre-printed in their heads...and there is nothing helpful in any of them. Let's go. I've got to talk to you."

The two men dart out the back door and into the alley. The Mayor starts the car and drives out onto the street. A few reporters spot his car and chase after it, but he guns it and leaves them behind. "Hallelujah!" he says. Rain continues to bounce off the windshield as daylight breaks through the night, promising Philadelphians a miserable day as they awaken.

Marshall's phone rings again.

"Shut that damn thing off," Mayor White orders.

One commercial street they drive along begins coming alive. Small diners and bagel shops light up to prepare for breakfast restaurants. Mostly black women dressed in hospital worker's garb wait at a bus stop to make it in time to begin an eight a.m. shift. The Mayor points at a movie theater.

"That was where that black woman got mugged and killed last week, with everyone watching."

"I know," Ed Marshall replies.

"She left five kids."

Marshall shrugs.

The Mayor turns into a side street that is mostly abandoned. One empty lot has been turned into a junkyard surrounded by a barbed-wire-topped chain link fence. Tires line up, strung along the fence as if to block incoming gunfire. The colorful graffiti that covers them is the only brightness in an otherwise morose area.

"This block has at least four shooting galleries that send out drugged-up monsters to rape, mug, and murder," he says.

"Is this a proposed crime tour of the city to generate revenue?" D.A. Marshall asks sarcastically.

"No, this is a tour of our careers...the end of them. More importantly, it is a tour of the future of the entire city if we don't do something quick and bold."

The D.A. blandly answers, "There's not much anyone can do without funds."

"Exactly," the Mayor replies. "That's why if I don't become Governor and open up some purse strings, shift some money from the State's Porky Pig projects, this city is sunk," he goes on. "And the first step in being elected is being nominated by my party, which, at this juncture, looks like it's going the way of the Titanic."

"What can I do?"

"Hang on a minute. Enjoy the scenery. I want to show you something."

The Mayor and District Attorney drive silently. Theirs was a perfect example of a marriage of opposites. Everything went well between the two men while the Mayor was able to finance his District Attorney's war on organized crime. As their belts tightened their different backgrounds and philosophies of city management snaked to the forefront. Mayor White's common background, growing up among people who were able to bob and weave and be inventive to get ahead clashed with Ed Marshall's privileged patrician background, where he set a path forward with what the Mayor considered to be blinders, unable to think out of the box or compromise on his methods.

They finally stop at a street in the heart of what once was Philadelphia's Little Italy. All the stores that used to be vibrant and alive with patrons are shuttered. Trash litters the streets. Posters and graffiti cover practically every inch of brick and the metal roll down gates that protect windows.

"All we need is tumbleweed to declare this a ghost town," Mayor White mutters, mostly to himself. He pulls to a stop in front of a store with accordion gates and black painted windows behind them. He turns to Ed Marshall. "Want to get out and walk here?"

"Are you crazy?"

"If you recall, there was a time when you could walk this block any time of the day or night and feel safe."

"Nothing comes without a price," Marshall replies.

"It was lively, with cafes, restaurants...tourists."

Marshall looks at the store with the accordion gates. "...Mobsters."

"Mobsters who, if I remember correctly, kept things in order here."

The D.A.'s voice takes on a bitter tone, "If you balance things out, though, everyone comes out way ahead with them gone. They were more of a threat to the fabric of our society than a few shuttered businesses."

"Try telling that to the people who owned those businesses."

D.A. Ed Marshall continues to stare at the storefront. It burns in his gut that all his efforts to incarcerate the withered old titular head of the social club behind the gate and the city's Cosa Nostra organization, Filippo Alessi, have failed. His face flushes bright scarlet. "That fuckin' old man, Alessi," he mutters, then out loud says, "Talk about a Teflon Don."

The two men drive silently again to City Hall, where a crowd of reporters has already formed and awaits them. A police officer who guards the barricade recognizes the Mayor's car and helps clear the way for him to drive right to the building's front door. Four officers surround Mayor White and Ed Marshall to escort them into the building while another cop drives off in the car to park it.

Inside City Hall, the Mayor and D.A. nod to people as they walk toward the Mayor's

office. The Mayor breaks the icy silence they've maintained since they left Little Italy. "You rose with me to this point through hard work and dependability, and if I go further, my chair is waiting for you."

"I am aware of that."

"But, by the same token, you must take the bad with the good. If I sink, you do too."

They enter the Mayor's outer office, where his secretary frantically jumps from phone call to phone call, pushing buttons, repeating that the Mayor's not in, and typing in messages. She looks to the Mayor for a signal that she can send calls to him. He answers her silent plea with, "Under no circumstances am I to be disturbed," and continues into his private office with Ed Marshall. A *"JONATHON WHITE FOR GOVERNOR"* sign hangs on one wall. The Mayor points to his seat behind the desk. "Go on, Edward, sit there. Get the feel of it."

Edward Marshall hesitantly sits in the Mayor's chair high-backed burgundy leather swivel chair. He fidgets nervously. Mayor White sits across from him in a guest armchair.

Mayor White continues to speak, "I've given the situation a lot of thought, and have decided that formula solutions to the chaotic crime problem we have won't work. These are times that call for alternative measures."

"I still don't see—"

"So far, I've only found two viable solutions to bring the level of violence in this city down quickly. The first is to request National Guard troops to patrol our hottest spots."

"It could work."

The Mayor went on, "The problem is that I have kids myself, and the idea of having them eat a hamburger with G.I. Joe watching over them instead of Ronald McDonald, is abhorrent. I absolutely refuse."

"That leaves number two?"

"The best alternative measure, as far as I can see...is to bring back Organized Crime."

D.A. Marshall leaps forward. "WHAT?!!"

"Bring back Organized Crime," Mayor White continues in a calm that contrasts sharply with D.A. Marshall's agitation. "...On a limited basis, of course."

Edward Marshall grabs his briefcase, ready to leave. "You've lost your mind."

"Sit the fuck down!"

When Edward Marshall, cowed by the Mayor's vehemence, begins to sit again, the Mayor moves toward him while pointing at the guest's chair he himself just vacated. "No, there!"

Edward Marshall complies, while the Mayor sits in his rightful place. "You need big balls to sit in this chair, Edward. Grow them or get fuck out of the game."

Marshall bristles, but remains silent.

"It makes perfect sense to me that if we were to make some kind of arrangement with one of the Mafiosi who managed to escape prosecution," the Mayor says, "look the other way on some harmless enterprises, like gambling..."

"I don't believe I'm hearing this."

"Just imagine if they could re-establish enough influence in their area to keep it free of violent crime again?" He went on, "If they could do that, we could concentrate whatever forces we do have in other areas. Citizens all around the city would feel safe, and we'd be heroes...I'd probably become Governor; you, Mayor." He concluded with, "Everyone's a winner"

"It's insane."

"No, just desperate," Mayor White replies"

"Do you realize how much I fought to get Organized Crime cleaned up? How much of my blood and soul I left in our courtrooms to give our city a better legacy than being known as one of the main Mafia centers of the country?"

As Philadelphia's District Attorney, Edward Marshall had launched an aggressive and relentless war on organized crime, unequaled by that of any American city in history. Robert F. Kennedy was his hero as U.S. Attorney General, and he modeled his assault on the mob after the President's brother's single minded pursuit of Jimmy Hoffa and other organized crime figures. The difference was he made sure he wouldn't be assassinated during his effort. Now, the suggestion by Mayor White that his work might be unraveled is dizzying.

The Mayor goes on, "Even if it's just for enough time for the polls to change and to get me that nomination."

Unable to control himself any longer, Edward Marshall begins pacing in front of Mayor White's desk. "Aside from this idea of yours being against every principle I…we…stand for, if we are discovered to have done that our careers will be ruined."

"If things stay the way they are, our careers...and this city...are ruined anyway."

"No, it's too risky. Count me out."

"There's no out here, Edward. You are either on my side or against me. No middle ground. Make your choice now."

"You know it won't work."

"How do we know unless we try?"

"It's appalling."

"I agree. And, I've got the perfect candidate: Don Filippo Alessi."

"Alessi?!" Ed Marshall snaps. "Think of what that man has

been responsible for in his lifetime."

"That's history. Our problems are today."

The District Attorney's voice amps up, "And what am I supposed to do, waltz in and offer him a deal over cappuccino?"

"If necessary. Just make sure you do it quickly...before you're off to Hawaii."

Ed Marshall is scheduled to leave for Honolulu in thirty-six hours for a convention of district attorneys from across the country. For him it is more important than anything he's ever done or will do. He's scheduled to be a keynote speaker, which will give him a launch pad for a future national political run. "I give up."

"Then you will take care of it?"

Defeated, Ed Marshall turns on his cell phone and dials as he replies, "No, but I have just the person who will."

3

Still out of sorts, Nicole Gianetti finally walks into her office at the Philadelphia *Assistant District Attorney's Office for Consumer Fraud*. Through her ride on the bus had her shoved and squashed and irritated, it was her need for a better relationship that had permeated her thoughts. When she was pushed body to body with a handsome man who smiled down at her, she'd had the urge to stay pressed against him; to feel the heat rise in her as she'd imagined it would in him. She had almost lost herself in her own sensuality when she'd looked beyond him to view another newspaper heading about the previous night's massacre. Sexual luxury had slipped from her body in an instant.

Now, back to the real world, Nicole downs more coffee from a pot that has been prepared earlier by one of the other A.D.A.s then immerses herself in paperwork. Then her cell phone rings…

* * * *

Edward Marshall sits across from Nicole Gianetti in a crowded City Hall chop house. He acknowledges people with a smile, a nod of his head, or a slight wave of his hand even as his conversation with Nicole progresses.

"No! Absolutely not!" she snaps.

Marshall responds as he waves to a councilman leaving. "Nicole, just be reasonable."

"Reasonable? It's a shitty assignment, and what's more, Edward, darling, it's fucking insulting!"

"Shhh, lower your voice."

"You know, Edward, you're a real prick."

"You haven't complained about it before," Marshall says with a forced smile.

"I put up with the jokes about Italians and the Mafia all through college. *'Hear about the new Italian car called the Mafia?'* she says bitterly. *"The hood is behind the wheel and the body is in the trunk.'* I fucking hate those animals more than you do!"

D.A. Marshall smiles again. "My favorite is the one about why you don't want to assign a female detective to follow a Mafia suspect."

"Don't you dare!"

"Just kidding," Marshall quickly says.

Nicole shoots him an impatient look. Being Italian has always been a burden to her, and she is sure it is in large part because of the overwhelming control Italians had over the business of organized crime.

"I even went to work in your shitty office because private law firms gave me the blues about Mafia ties," she continues. "Tell the truth, Edward, didn't your office check with more diligence when you saw an Italian name on my application? Especially one from South Philly?"

She pushes aside her uneaten Cobb salad.

Ed Marshall begins to pick meat out of the salad. "You know we have to be careful."

"But not if my name was Kelly or Schwartz. I thought you were different."

"I am. It's just that—"

"That all of us Italians have a secret Mafia connection? Is that it?"

"If you'd only stop being so goddamned paranoid," Marshall lectures.

"I have every fucking right to be!" What had made things worse for Nicole Gianetti through her law school and early work years was that the jokes and suspicion of her because she was Italian had driven her to get away from the nasty trick her genes had played on her and try to defy them and change herself: dyed her hair lighter from its natural Mediterranean black; changed her clothing to WASP dull; even wore eyeglasses she didn't need. While it made her less noticeable to those who would tease her, though in a seemingly good natured way, it inspired the thugs outside her neighborhood social club to jeer at her in an ugly, much more sexual and hurtful way than anything she'd experienced before. She not only blamed them for being the kind of Italians she was teased or mistrusted over, but hated them for their crude, cutting treatment when she'd tried to fit into the larger world beyond the ethnic ghetto she occupied with them.

Ed Marshall continued in a more compassionate tone, "What I was going to say was that I trust you. Especially now, with me having to be away at the Hawaiian thing...you're really the only one I do trust."

"And I'm Italian."

"And you're Italian. And you're a female...a beautiful one at that. Alessi might be more apt to talk to someone he doesn't feel threatened by; who he –"

"Identifies with? Well, Edward, the answer is no. No! No! NO!"

*   *   *   *

Nicole walks along the same Little Italy street where Mayor White and D.A. Marshall had parked that morning. She pulls her collar up against the cold and wind that moved in directly behind the rainy front of the previous day. She passes three young punks hanging out in a building's doorway. They eye her as if surveying her for an assault or robbery. Nicole nervously clutches a can of pepper spray in one gloved hand and a small electric stun gun in the other. Thinking she shouldn't have worn her Coach shoulder bag, she hugs it close to her body, protecting it with her elbow.

She finally stops in front of the store with the accordion gate. She quickly switches the stun gun for a paper with an address that she checks against the stick-on numbers on the painted black door then switches paper for stun gun even faster. After a quick look over her shoulder at the young punks she sticks her arm through the gate and knocks on the window with the pepper spray can. When she gets no response she bangs the pepper spray can on the glass again, and waits some more.

Nicole is about to leave when a peephole in the door opens and an eye appears in it. The eyeball looks from side to side then focuses on her. A tobacco-roughened voice asks, "Whattaya wan'?"

"Nice greeting," Nicole says. "I'm looking for Filippo Alessi."

"Who?"

"Don Filippo?"

"Who you?"

"I have to speak with him."

"You got a name?"

"He won't recognize it," Nicole says with exasperation. "Would you please let me in? It's cold out here, and I know he will want to speak with me."

The peephole shuts. Nicole moves around to keep herself warm while and keeps an eye on the young punks. She hears the sound of a plane overhead and looks up, cursing Edward Marshall and the plane that could be the one taking him to Hawaii. The fact that it is headed north is lost on her. Becoming more irritated with each passing minute, she knocks even harder, waits a couple of seconds then knocks again. Suddenly she hears a number of locks being opened from the inside and the door opens slowly. A rough-looking short man in an open leather jacket with a bright purple bulky sweater under it, steps outside.

"Maah, what's you hurry?" the old man asks. He cautiously opens the gate locks, looks around, lets Nicole squeeze through the small opening he allows, and immediately relocks it. He ushers Nicole into the dim old interior furnished with castoffs; a green leather couch patched with grey duct tape; a stained blue cut velvet chair. The place smells as old as the occupants with overtones of diNobli smoke and espresso. A few tough-looking seniors sit around playing cards. Every one of them is wearing the same sweater as the old man who let her in, but in all different bright colors. They suspiciously eye Nicole as she follows her guide to the rear of the room, where Don Filippo, a gnome of an old man, watches the final minutes of a soap opera. She stands impatiently waiting for the don to acknowledge her, but he continues to watch the television.

Without looking away from the screen, Don Filippo says, "You know, soap operas are good to watch. You could learn a lot about real life from them."

Nicole just smiles impatiently.

Don Filippo continues to speak while watching the television show. "I know you?"

"No. May I sit? I'd like to speak with you for a few minutes."

"Reporter?"

"No. District Attorney's Office."

Don Filippo lets out an impatient sigh then shuts the television with a remote device and finally turns away from the screen. "I got a lawyer; you could call him. Youse should know I got nothing to say."

"You don't need an attorney. I've been asked to come here and discuss a...a...an arrangement with you."

"Aspetto."

Don Filippo waves to the old man who guided Nicole. "Funzi, *vene ca,* an' bring 'the thing' with you."

Suddenly worried, Nicole looks around at the hardened

faces. Is *the thing* a gun? Funzi brings an attaché case to the table, which he sets down and opens. Inside are electronic bug-detecting devices. He lifts an antenna, turns some dials then checks a meter.

"It's okay, you could talk," Funzi says then departs with the equipment.

"Now, *bellezza, sei Italiana?*"

Nicole's face drops at the last thing she ever wanted to hear. Though she doesn't speak her native language, she has a rudimentary understanding of simple words, like "Are you Italian." The lawyer in her allows her to recover immediately and without acknowledging Don Filippo's question make her pitch to him. The authorities, she says, without mentioning the Mayor or D.A., are willing to look the other way on non-violent criminal activity, like gambling, if he will solidify those loyal to him in his Little Italy neighborhood, and bring back the peaceful environment that had existed in the past. Don Filippo sits quietly throughout her proposal.

"...We can work out exact parameters if you agree in principle," Nicole says at the conclusion of her speech.

The don only smiles.

"Did I say something amusing?" she asks.

"Yes. It is funny to me," the don replies. "You people hounded us like we were disease-carrying animals. What did you think you would have once you destroyed us, no more crime? You got what you wanted, now live with it."

"Please," Nicole says. "If not for the city, then think of yourselves. I can get you some major—"

"Why did they send you?"

"Because they wanted to—"

"No, you. Why did they send you? Because you're Italian?"

Nicole hesitates then finally nods slowly.

"An' that bothers you?"

"Yes."

"That is too bad."

The don pauses. He stares at Nicole as if he's able to see and examine inside her. "I'm sorry," he says, "but I can't help you. You see how we live. We're old men. We lock ourselves in here, and my guys go home at night in packs, with guns...all legal, of course. I'm lucky; I live upstairs an' never have to go out. There's nothing I could do."

A defeated Nicole just sits for a few moments, eyes downcast, trying to think of a next move. If there was only something she could say; something to convince this old man and not have to return to the office as a failure.

With a wave of his bony hand, Don Filippo summons Funzi to the table then tells Nicole, "Go, before it gets dark an' the real animals come out. My men'll walk you to your car.

Saddened, Nicole prepares to leave. The old don gets up and hugs her, pulls back to stare into her eyes, then hugs her again. She is taken aback at first then hugs him back.

"Come back earlier one day," the don says, with more warmth than he's shown since she arrived. "We'll have lunch...watch a soap opera together."

Nicole smiles wanly. "Yes."

As she turns toward the door, Don Filippo sayss, "Aah, but, *bellezza*, if you really want help, I think I know just the person who could do it."

4

Larry Bellino plays cards at a small table on the tier of the prison he's been locked up in for the past six years. The bleak gray cinderblock walls and steel bars contrast to the dapper neatness of Larry's handsome Mediterranean features, expensive grey sweat suit, sparkling white sneakers, and air of authority. His card partners are his boyish-looking nephew, Anthony, who they call Trickster, and Vincent "Boom Boom" Rizza, a muscular former cruiserweight prizefighter in his late forties. Most of the cells on that tier are empty. Andrea Bocelli sings in the background.

In a laundry area at the end of the tier Johnny "J.C." Coniglio…tough-looking and overweight, but with a likeable demeanor…stirs spaghetti in a washing machine heated by two home-made electrical stingers hanging into it to boil the water. J.C. scurries into the first empty cell to stir garlic and oil that is slow simmering on a makeshift stove of a cookie tin that has been retrofitted in one of the prison's shops with a clothes dryer heating element embedded in cement and a connecting wire plugged into the wall. He sniffs the garlic and smiles like he's reached Nirvana.

"Another two minutes, Larry," J.C. calls.

Larry answers immediately, "Good, I'm starving."

Trickster chimes in, "Me too, J.C., my old pal."

"You're always starving, you little fuck," J.C. says. "I thought I ate a lot, but you gotta have two assholes."

"I'll show youse who's the two assholes," Trickster replies, and slams down a King of Spades on the table. "Take that!"

Larry laughs. "You wanna have a heart?" he says. "That's the third time you played that same card."

"You kidding?" Boom Boom asks. "I didn't notice. You did that Trickster?"

"Me? Boom Boom, would I do that?"

"I let it go by the second time you played it," Larry says, "just to show you I could beat you no matter what you did."

"Oh, yeah," Trickster says, and reaches over to toss all the cards into a jumbled mess. "Now, prove it." He rushes over to J.C., hovering over the food. "Food ready for the champ?"

"You said 'chump,' right?" J.C. asks.

"I'll kill that nephew of yours one day, Larry, I swear," Boom Boom says. "You know what that little fuck did to me this morning?"

"I can only imagine, Boom."

"He glued my flip-flops to the floor during the night. I nearly killed myself when I got outta bed and tried to walk. Hit my fuckin' head on the bunk, an' everything."

Larry laughs. "Why do you think we call him Trickster?"

A prison guard walks down the tier toward the men. J.C. closes the washing machine, puts a trash pail over the cookie-tin stove and sits on it.

"Sure smells like South Philly to me," the guard says.

"Nah, it's your imagination," Larry answers. "It's just us

guineas, hoss. You know we always smell like garlic."

"I sure hope you guys are saving some of that good-smelling imaginary shit for me."

"C'mon, hoss," Larry answers, "you know when we get something we always take care of you."

"Well, today you can give me a double, Bellino, 'cause you got a lawyer's visit an' won't be around for awhile."

J.C. calls to the guard, "Hey, you wanna take a quick walk before the macaroni you're imagining gets too soft for us to make believe we're eatin'."

The guard smiles at J.C. "I like that...respect."

"...An' before this make believe fire under here burns my ass to a fuckin' make believe crisp."

"Okay, okay, I'm outta here," the guard says. "But before I go, you gotta go with me Bellino...visiting duds quick as you could, so I could get back here and chow down some of that imaginary *Eye-talian* food."

"Who is it? I'm not expecting anyone."

"Paper says a legal visit. Bring your papers."

Larry slips into a sharply pressed tan prison outfit, grabs an accordion envelope full of legal documents, and follows the guard through dark, Gothic prison hallways while wondering who could be visiting him. He has no family left to come see him and he's dismissed his attorney, figuring that all the appeals in the world wouldn't get the court to accept his innocence of what he'd been charged with, and that he had passed halfway through his sentence and was on his way out of the forest instead of going into it. They reached a section with small private offices used for legal visits, which had windows, but supposedly no video observation or sound system to record conversations. Larry believes they are full of shit and conducts himself in there as if the authorities can see every motion and hear every word.

"Okay, that room there, Bellino," the guard says and proceeds to pat Larry down from head to toe. "You're good. Have fun."

Larry opens the door to find Nicole Gianetti waiting at a table inside. "Hey, hoss, I think you got the wrong guy or the wrong room."

The guard checks his paper. "No, sir, Bellino. That pretty lady's in there for you."

"Who is she?"

"Lawyer?"

"Genius," Larry says. "Wait here; don't leave."

"Nine years shouldn't be long enough to make you afraid of girls."

Larry reopens the door to the legal room where Nicole sits. "Who are you?"

"Nicole Gianetti…"

"From?"

"Philadelphia D.A.'s Office, but—"

Larry slams the door shut.

5

Nicole paces anxiously in her bedroom while on the phone to the Llikai Hotel in Honolulu, Hawaii. Since Edward Marshall has refused to answer her calls on his cell phone, desperation instead of reality has driven her to call the desk and hope he returns her message. Not to mention that she's imagined him not responding to calls while stretched out on a chaise lounge by the pool, ogling beauties in skimpy threads of fabric that substitute for real bathing suits. A desk clerk at the Llikai finally answers, and Nicole asks for Edward Marshall.

"Mr. Marshall is not in his room," the desk clerk replies dryly. "Would you like to leave a message?"

She was tempted to shout, *"Tell him to go fuck himself!"* but simply replied, "Just tell him that Nicole is trying to reach him, and that it's extremely important."

Nicole slams the photo of Ed Marshall on her dresser down on its face. "Fuck!"

* * * *

On downtown Walnut Street, two thieves run from a jewelry store they've just robbed at gunpoint and toward a waiting car. When the store's owner runs out after them, one of the thieves turns and fires shots at him. The store owner is hit and goes down, along with a woman shopper nearby. The getaway car takes off without a policeman in sight.

* * * *

Mayor White drops a newspaper onto his desk, then leans back and covers his eyes. The newspaper's headline reads: "KILLINGS UP -- MAYOR DOWN: PARTY BIGWIGS MEET TO WITHDRAW GOV ENDORSEMENT." His secretary stands alongside the desk, eyeing the newspaper headline and waiting for instructions. The Mayor stands, walks to the poster announcing his running for Governor, and angrily rips it off the wall. He screams at his secretary, "Get me Marshall, now!" She hurries out then returns minutes later.

"D.A. Marshall's message box is full on his phone," the secretary says, "and the desk clerk at the hotel only said he would take a message."

The Mayor flings the newspaper halfway across the room. "Fuck!"

* * * *

District Attorney Edward Marshall sits alongside three professional law enforcement people and an empty chair on the stage of the hotel's convention auditorium. A huge sign above them reads *LAW ENFORCEMENT U.S.A.* At the podium, a young black police commissioner from Detroit, who left the chair behind him empty, finishes a discussion on sensitivity to Muslim citizens

29

when trying to prevent terrorist attacks. *Fuck'em all*, Ed Marshall thinks, while sneaking a glimpse at his watch. The police commissioner ends his speech and returns to his seat to obligatory applause. He is replaced at the podium by the current head of the Public Safety Forum Group, a fortyish brunette with her hair in a tight knot and in a simple but obviously expensive gray dress who Marshall has classified as a two bagger: one over her head and one over yours in case hers falls off. *But she does have a great body and absolutely stunning legs.*

"Thank you Commissioner Binghamton," the moderator says.

Ed Marshall stares at her ass and legs some more, pictures rubbing his fingers along them, and contemplates asking her to accompany him for a drink afterwards.

The moderator continues, "Now, from the City of Brotherly Love, a man instrumental in cleaning up Organized Crime: Philadelphia's District Attorney, Edward Marshall."

More applause as Ed Marshall strides toward the podium. He makes sure to take Hot Legs' hand in his. It feels surprisingly dull and dry, and puts doubt in his mind about whether she'd be worth pursuing; worth having those dry hands creating painful friction on his private flesh. He turns to the podium as she leaves the stage.

"As I am sure you all know, we in Philadelphia have recently become victim to a rash of violence," Marshall begins. "While that violence, which, you may rest assured we will put an end to shortly, is terrible, it does not compare to the deep destruction of society attributed to Organized Crime..."

* * * *

Nicole Gianetti is awakened from a deep sleep by her cell phone ringing. She reaches for it on her bare black nightstand, which has only a stick lamp and digital clock to accompany it. Still more in a sleep than out of it, she answers, "Mmmm, hello." After getting a response, she says, "Oh, Edward. What time is it?"

"You must stop calling me," Marshall says on the phone.

"That was yesterday."

"That is beside the point. I told you *I* would call *you*."

"Edward! What the fuck are you doing, sawing off a limb with me on it?"

"Not at all," Marshall says unconvincingly. "We will speak when I return."

"Bullshit!"

"The mission you were given is just as distasteful for me as it is for you."

"I somehow doubt that," Nicole answers.

"...But we will also share huge rewards if we succeed," Ed Marshall says. "Remember, as I move up, so do you."

Nicole answers with the same disappointment that has gripped her since she'd left Larry Bellino at the prison. "Neither of us is going anywhere, Edward, since this so called *mission* is dead. I went to see Aless—"

"Nicole, for Christ's sake! This is still a telephone we are speaking on. No names, please!"

"Yes, but—"

"No buts!" the D.A. snaps. "I'm getting calls...well, let's just say I'm getting pressure."

"Did you tell *you know who* not to call also?" she asks, sarcastically referring to Mayor White.

Edward Marshall remains impatiently. Nicole can almost feel him gritting his teeth. "Edward, that old man sent me to someone else, who won't even talk to me. I—"

"Do whatever you have to," he replies. "You are totally in charge. Please, Nicole, quickly."

"But—"

"But nothing. We will speak again when I return...not before."

Nicole stares at a phone that CLICKS OFF at the other end.

6

Once again, Nicole is in front of Don Filippo's club and knocks on the window through the gates. Cold wind sluices up her legs under her dress, making her wish she'd worn pants. Something inside had told her that the don was old fashioned enough to be turned off by her approaching him dressed like a female trying to climb the modern business world by, in his mind, dressing like a man; she presses her thighs together to keep them warmer. Her nose feels frozen enough to snap off. She waits more patiently, though still nervous about being attacked by neighborhood punks and hanging on to her spray and zapper, until Funzi, wearing another of the same colorful sweaters, this time in red, opens the door.

"*Ciao, bella,*" he greets her warmly.

She smiles.

* * * *

Nicole sits anxiously waiting. She picks at her cuticle as the door opens and Larry steps inside, carrying no papers. He's got a big-time attitude, and silently sits across the table from her and stares. As if moving completely on their own, from instinct rather than intention, his eyes seem to lick her from her hair to her breasts and up again, then quickly go back to their controlled stare.

"If you look at females like that on the outside, you'll be back in before you can unzip your pants."

"Who said I was going anywhere?" Larry states more than asks. "I only agreed to talk to you because the old man said I should."

"Charming too. Your record didn't list that quality."

Larry snaps back, "Does it list how you framed me?"

"I don't frame people."

"Or, how my wife and father both died during these last nine years?"

"I'm sorry," Nicole replies, "but I was in high school when you went to trial."

"Okay, smartass," Larry says, "let's cut the small talk. Get to the point, tell me what you wanna tell me, an' let me get back to my cell."

Larry and Nicole go at it for more than an hour, she trying to convince him of why it is in his interest to leave prison and recapture his area, and he knocking each reason down with bitterness and attitude. Nicole listens to his protestations of innocence, but tries not to believe him. She's convinced that his arguments are what he's learned since he was a youth growing up in the midst of Mafiosi; it was part of the tradition to lie to authorities. It was part of the culture of saying FBI stood for "Forever Bothering Italians," as if their organization had inducted Lithuanians and Turks instead of limiting it to those whose ancestry went back to the Kingdom of the Two Sicilies.

On the other hand, the fact that he'd lost the people closest to him during that time was true, but she reminds herself it was his fault alone. No one had forced him to follow a life of crime. She'd fought back against that tradition that had permeated her neighborhood growing up. He could have also. She struggles to focus on the important fact: she needs his help in order for her to survive in her world. She sips more of the miserable prison coffee then continues, "You would save six years of your life."

"I already done nine. I'm more out than in."

"Don't be a shmuck," she snaps. "Six years is still six years. This macho toughguy act is worth total bullshit!"

"We'll see what's bullshit and what's not." He stands and starts for the door.

"No, wait!" she quickly cries.

Larry shoots her a *fuck you* look then continues to open the door.

Nicole's attitude softens as she panics that she will fail. "Please."

"Okay, Monty Hall, how much do you want a deal?" Larry asks. "And how much power do you have to make one?"

Nicole answers him honestly, "How much do I want it? My ass could be grass...dead, brown, crispy grass...for participating in this idiotic scheme," she says. "And, because of that, I can do whatever I see fit."

"No approvals needed?"

"Just me."

"Okay, you want a deal? Here's my deal..."

Larry Bellino sets forth a list of demands that under normal circumstances she would have laughed at and walked out. But nothing about this situation even approaches normal. He tells her he wants others released with him; three of his co-defendants: his sister's son, Anthony "Trickster" Scala...

In a prison television room, Trickster toys with wires behind a television playing a soap opera, while other inmates keep their eyes on him and the screen, and one is posted as a lookout. Suddenly, the show they are watching turns to static, then to a porno flick. The inmates celebrate quietly, so not to draw the attention of guards. They smile, pat Trickster on the back and give him high fives as he makes his way past them to his seat.

"...Trickster's my nephew. He's a pain in the ass, but he's my blood and he keeps my life interesting," he says. "Also, J.C., Johnny Coniglio..."

Outside his cell, J.C. trades cigarettes with another inmate in kitchen whites, who gives him contraband prison food that he'd stuffed into all his pockets, sleeves, and even inside his pants and socks. J.C. hides the food in and under his locker and under his bed then turns over a cheese sandwich that he's grilling on the institution's wall lamp.

"J.C. keeps me fed, even in here. He does wonders on the outside with real food."

"And Rizza?" Nicole asks.

"Boom Boom? To make sure I stay alive."

Nicole hates being on the short end of negotiations with him and feels compelled to make somewhat of an argument. "I don't understand why you *need* them. I'm sure you have other friends outside who can help you."

He looks at her half-smiling, as if he understands her

obligatory act of resistance. "Take it or leave it." He adds that those three all have appeals pending, so all she has to do is arrange bail pending a hearing, and that he would have his attorney file one so he could get bail too.

Nicole wishes she could smack the smirk of his face.

7

Nicole watches from a parked Ford SUV she's rented as Larry, Trickster, J.C., and Boom Boom exit from the prison gate into the brilliant sunshine. The men look around appreciatively, sniff the air, congratulate and hug each other. They look to her like high school teammates who have just won a big game. She has to remind herself that they are not innocent teens, but hardened criminals, and grimaces at their joy. Thinking *If I'm going to cut my own throat, I might as well do it all the way,* Nicole shifts into drive and pulls up in front of the group. She rolls down the passenger window. "Get in."

Larry climbs into the front. Trickster is the first to enter through the back door.

"Where's the girls?" Trickster asks. "Man, even in 'Once Upon a Time in America,' they bring DeNiro a naked broad in a coffin when he gets out of the can."

Nicole just groans. She instantly believes Trickster is someone even a mother can't love. She wonders how Larry Bellino, who is so grounded and seemingly stable for a pathological criminal can spend any time with him at all. The other two, the muscle bound Rizza, who tells Trickster to shut up, and the fat cook Coniglio, are both obviously uncomfortable around her and quiet as a result, with just a grunt or nod as a greeting, don't allow her to get an impression of them as individuals; just maintain what she knows about them from their records and law enforcement notes.

She glances at Larry, who stares out the side window. Even in prison, she thinks, his hair, thick and black with gray streaks throughout, is always perfectly groomed. "Fasten your seat belt," she says. "It's the law now."

"Arrest me," he replies.

I can see this is going to be a joy, she thinks, and wonders what her next career choice will be.

As they pass skeletons of abandoned construction sites that ruin the landscape's former beauty, Larry opines bitterly. "I don't need a newspaper to see you guys cleaned up the construction industry."

"Yes, and proud of it."

Larry laughs sarcastically then asks, "Proud of what?" He lectures that the biggest success of the war on that business was not to clean it up but to put more people out of work, cheapen the value of the area, and congratulate each other on their success. "What was the motive?" he wonders out loud, "dropouts from private business completion who want to control every bit of other people's lives and business, or getting rid of people like me who can make more money than any of you do?"

"It has nothing to do with money," Nicole answers.

"Then why do you show juries photos of our closets full of clothes they can't afford? Furs and sexy outfits bought for our beautiful wives and girlfriends that men in the juries can only drool over and never have? Or the kind females in the juries...or prosecutors...are jealous of?"

"Believe me, I'm not jealous of any idiotic female who

would sleep with people like you," she replies with irritation. That brings chuckles from the back seat.

Trickster says, "Somebody's got her thong in a knot."

"Asshole," Nicole snaps.

"Shut up," Larry tells his nephew. Boom Boom slaps Trickster on the back of the head. Larry goes back to attacking Nicole, "Yeah, none of you are jealous once you frame guys like us then get'em out of your sight."

"Pu-leeze," Nicole groans. "Remind me to stop and get polish for your halo."

Larry tells her to forget the polish but stop by his old barber in South Philly. He says they all have nine years of jailhouse stink to get off. Boom Boom finally speaks up, saying, "I second that." J.C. chimes in with, "Me too." Trickster tells them that he doesn't need it as badly as they do; that he smells like roses.

"Yeah," J.C. says, "after a billygoat shits'em out."

How can he worry about going to a barber? Nicole wonders about Larry Bellino. *He looks like he just came from a GQ photo shoot. What a fucked up bunch.*

Before going to the barber shop, Larry tells Nicole to stop at Holy Cross Cemetery, on Bailey Road. While the others remain in the car, Larry walks to the graves of his father and wife. He stays for a time, removing weeds and kissing the tombstones as if he can make contact with his deceased loved ones through them. Everyone in the car is quiet, even after Larry returns.

"Let's go," Larry says.

Nicole pulls up to the address Larry gave her to find a

shuttered barber shop among other closed stores. The motionless red, white, and blue striped barber pole is an incongruous splash of color on an otherwise gray location, making the surrounding sullenness look even worse. Larry stares out at the sign, at the small hanging barber pole that no longer rotates, at the padlock on the roll down gate. He is visibly upset, which the others in the back seem to sense.

"Things change," J.C. says.

Larry murmurs, "Yeah."

Nicole notes that his release from prison into the outside world has changed his steady anger that gave him vibrancy to a palpable cloak of sadness.

The last stop Larry demands is at Don Filippo's social club. He and his men walk with Nicole down the same street she has traveled twice before. Since darkness is falling fast, there is more street scum hanging around than usual—hookers, pimps, and other thugs. Some hang around looking for trouble, some make obvious drug deals, others flash knives to threaten prey that has unwittingly wandered onto the block. When the thugs look toward Larry and Nicole, Larry and his men challengingly stare straight back at them. Nicole pulls the pepper spray from her bag.

"What the hell is that?" Larry asks.

"Pepper spray."

"Put that away. It's goddamn embarrassing."

Nicole slips the can back into her bag. She suddenly feels the power of having four men backing her and straightens up to stare back at the punks also. They stop at a spot next to Don Filippo's club that appears to be the center of the block's illegal activity. It is lit up from the inside with a red light. Larry nods toward a group of hookers outside, indicating to J.C. to go to them, which he does. J.C. puts an arm around the shoulders of two of the scantily clad females.

"Okay, my little sugarplums," J.C. says to them. "As of this minute, this neighborhood is verboten. Find another spot to peddle these delightful little asses of yours."

One of the girls says, "If you're looking to shake us down for a freebee, honey, it won't work. Everybody pays. Malik will make sure of that."

J.C. puts a hand on each of their asses and gives them a gentle shove. "Sorry, I'd love to spend the night proving youse wrong," he says, "but it's dispossess time. Go on, out, out..."

A pimp, leaning against a car notices and comes toward J.C. "Hey, motherfucker, you can't—" As the pimp reaches them, J.C. cuts his speech short without a word and tosses him over the roof of a car and into the street then asks the hooker, "Malik?" J.C.'s pimp toss sends Boom Boom and Larry into action. Boom Boom uses his martial arts expertise to fell four of the hoods that started towards them. Larry takes on one, hitting him with a garbage can cover. Trickster, spots one of the pimp's men pulling out an automatic weapon. He kicks him in the balls from behind then disarms him. He waves the gun at some of the other punks, who run off.

Meanwhile, Nicole knocks frantically on the window of Don Filippo's club then cowers against the gate, holding her pepper spray and stun gun in front of her for protection as bodies fly all around. Funzi finally opens up, and when he sees what's going on outside, calls into the club. "*Amici, vene ca*...an' bring the fuckin' bats!" He opens the gate and with a group of newly invigorated old men, all wearing the same sweaters as Funzi, which obviously *fell off the truck*, rush out and help Larry and his men pound the riffraff that had previously taken over their street.

When Larry sees most of those he's been fighting outside running away, he leads Boom Boom and J.C. into the red-lit store. Trickster stands by the side of the door, tripping those who run out so that the old men can beat them with bats before they escape. One well dressed pimp-type flies out over Trickster's foot, bringing a surprised expression from him. At the sound of footsteps running out of the store, he sticks his foot out again, only to trip Boom Boom, who gets up and, cursing, chases him down the block.

* * * *

In the midst of the mayhem, a midnight blue BMW passing by slows down but goes unnoticed by Larry and his men as they continue to congratulate themselves or stare with pride down the street they have recaptured.

The driver of the car is Carmine Favara, a street hood, who is approximately Larry's age. He slows down to focus on Larry and his men hugging each other and the old men who have helped them. As the group starts toward the club's door, Carmine takes note of Larry at the head of them taking Nicole by the arm to lead her inside. Carmine looks around the street, searching for remnants of the block's regulars. Seeing none, he steps on the gas and takes off.

* * * *

As Larry leaves Nicole to go to where Don Filippo stands, his arms wide open, Funzi puts an arm around Trickster. "Five minutes you guys are here," Funzi says, "an' already I feel twenty years younger."

"Try forty."

"That's why I love you, you little prick."

Nicole, still shaken, holds herself around and shudders. Funzi approaches her and in a warm grandfatherly way, asks if she's cold. He offers one of the brightly colored sweaters all the old men wear. He says he's got all colors in the back of the club. "You want one?" he asks. "They're free for you."

Her face just curls into a disgusted sneer as she walks away, while muttering, "They're all fucking insane."

Don Filippo summons Funzi, who hurries to him then brings out the suitcase device to check for electronic bugs, and begins sweeping the entire area. Boom Boom, J.C., and Trickster go off to affectionately hug and chat with the other old men in the club.

Before Don Filippo even gets the all clear from Funzi and his electronic gauges, he speaks to Larry. "Aaii, you look terrific. Jail agrees with you."

"Jail is jail," Larry says. "You either do the time, or let the time do you...and nothing's doing me." Unlike the don, he waits for an all-clear nod from Funzi before continuing, "Don Filippo, thank you so much for everything. I...we—"

"Don't thank me" Don Filippo replies. He waves Nicole over to him. She is still overwhelmed by the characters and action, and appears dazed as she obeys. "She's the one you should thank." When Nicole reaches the table, he tells her, "You did a good thing, taking this man outta jail. God's gonna bless you."

"I'm going to Hell."

The don continues, "You know he's innocent."

"Don't waste your breath on her," Larry jumps in. "She already bought the government's bullshit."

"No, no, she may be confused, but she's a good girl...*Italiana*. She's one of us."

Nicole starts, "I'm not —" but is interrupted by Don Filippo telling Larry, "Come on, let's go upstairs. Mimi's dying to see you." He turns to Nicole. "You too, come on. We'll order in some Chinks...for everybody down here too."

"Chinese food, if you don't mind."

Larry and Don Filippo chuckle at what they consider silly political correctness. Larry asks the old don, "Was I right about her, or what?"

8

At the same time that Nicole, Larry, and his men are at Don Filippo's, in a rundown old tenement apartment nearby with its windows boarded up, six naked females sit around a table packaging a huge pile of drugs into individual portion bags. They are exotic in the way of underground culture, with nipple rings, tattoos, and other piercings from eyebrows to vaginas. Their nails are clipped short; they all wear surgical masks.

One of the girls is Rachel, a fresh-as-dew pretty Latina, who looks especially young and nubile, and whose body jewelry has not yet progressed beyond a few earrings. Sully, a huge black overseer/guard watches over the girls as they work. Observing Sully and the girls is the sleazy- but tough-looking forty-eight year old boss of the operation, "Johnny Brown" Favara. He stands near a doorway that leads to another room, sipping espresso from a small *demitasse* cup. When Sully looks his way, Johnny Brown uses his head to motion the overseer to him.

"How's this new crew working out, Sully?"

"As good as any bunch of ho's, I guess.

"Guessing ain't good enough," Johnny says. "This new shit's too valuable and too powerful for them to fuck with. The last thing we need is an O.D. that leads back here."

Sully replies, "Unless it goes through those pretty titties, they ain't getting even a grain."

"Make sure it stays that way." He looks over at Rachel and can almost feel himself drooling. "Who's the new girl?"

"Sweet Pussy, I call that young thing," Sully says. "Her first day."

"Where'd you get her?

"Tito, from Chestnut Street, sent her over."

"How old is she?" Johnny asks. He feels his blood pulse more quickly and an erection forming.

"Who gives a fuck?" Sully answers. "Tito's responsible for her. That's all that counts." They had dealt in the harshest way with girls who had try to spirit drugs out of their operation, leaving some they felt wouldn't go to the feds marked with a scar to show their disloyalty, and those they couldn't depend on to keep their mouths shut dead. They'd shown no such confusion of policy with those who had recommended the girls, just murdering them. Tito would have had to be crazy, blinded by fantastic sex, or confident in Rachel to bet his life and recommend her.

When the door buzzer sounds, the girls get nervous and fidgety. Johnny puts his hand on a .357 in the back of his waistband. As he goes to check a television monitor, Sully yells to the girls, "Back to work, you silly bitches! You're on the big man's time now!" He looks at the screen showing the outside hallway, and tells Johnny, "It's your brother, Carmine." He then goes to the door and opens a variety of locks and bolts, the last of which is a police lock that releases a bolt that runs from the door into the floor. As he opens the door, an excited Carmine, who was just in the car outside Don Filippo's club, hurriedly enters and goes straight to Johnny Brown.

"John, John, you'll never guess who the fuck I just seen!"

"Elvis."

"No, really, Johnny, no kidding. It was Larry...Larry Bellino...and his whole crew...Boom Boom, J.C., even that little prick, Trickster."

"Get the fuck outta here," Johnny responds. "You must be using the shit you're supposed to be selling."

"No, Johnny, I would never do that. I know Larry. It was him...all of 'em, they chased everybody off their old block...hookers an' all."

Johnny Brown finally senses that his brother is serious, and asks incredulously, "Really?!"

"I swear. Then they went into Don Filippo's club," Carmine goes on. "Larry had some classy-looking bitch with him."

"That sure sounds like Larry, but they ain't due home for another six years?"

"I don't give a fuck when they're due, Johnny, he's here! This means big trouble. What the fuck do we do now?"

"Whoa, whoa, whoa!" Johnny says. "Fuckin' put a lid on it!" Though he struggles to maintain an outward appearance of calm, his insides twist in turmoil. The implications of Larry Bellino being out are larger than anyone, including his brother, is aware of. Johnny Brown grabs Carmine and drags him into the bedroom. "First, calm down and think. Are you absolutely sure it was them?"

"Fuck yeah!" Carmine says. "They wasn't a pigment of my imagination."

Johnny shoots his brother a *What are you, a fuckin' idiot?* look, then drops into a club chair, thinking, worrying, feeling like his stomach is dining on itself. Carmine shifts nervously, silently waiting for Johnny to say something, to tell him what they should do. After a thinking pause, Johnny speaks, but more to himself, to hear his own thoughts, than to Carmine.

"It don't make sense...nobody gets out early unless they're a rat, an' Larry ain't the kinda guy to rat." But could he be sure, he wonders? After guys like bosses Ralph Natale in his city and Bonanno head honcho Joe Massino in New York, he wouldn't swear for anyone. What he does know, however, is that appeals of convictions don't work for mob guys, and especially could not in Larry's case. Appeals have degenerated to where they are decided more on who you are than what your issues are, he tells himself, and Larry and his crew are not the favored *who*.

"What the fuck is going on?" he asks himself out loud. He turns to Carmine, "Get out in the street an' start dropping the word around that Larry's home early, an' that he could be a rat...not that he *is*, but that he *could be. Capisce?*"

"Oh, man, Johnny, if he—"

"Shut the fuck up an' do what I tell you!" Johnny yells. "Meanwhile, I'll get on the horn to my connection, an' get the whole scoop. Now, get out!"

Carmine leaves. Johnny thinks for awhile, tossing around questions and options around in his head till it pounds. He then gets up and goes to the doorway, where he motions for Sully, who immediately comes to him.

"Shut down for today," Johnny says. "Check out all the bitches except the new one. Send her to me."

Sully smiles a broad, lecherous smile. He goes to the table where the girls work. "Okay, that's it for today. We'll do the routine one at a time." He tells Rachel, "You, Sweet Pussy, go in the other room to the boss man."

Rachel stares blankly at Sully, then gets up and goes to the bedroom where Johnny Brown waits. When she hesitates at the doorway, Johnny surveys every inch of her naked skin, shiny with semi-perspiration and supple with youth. He calls her with a crooked forefinger. She slowly goes to him. "My name is Johnny Brown. You know who I am?"

Rachel nods.

"What's your name?"

Rachel answers in a low, timid voice that barely makes it through the drug-filtering mask she still wears, "Rachel."

"Rachel," Johnny repeats, letting his tongue linger on the final l sound. "You know what the routine is, to make sure you go out of here clean?"

With no emotion in her eyes, Rachel nods her understanding.

Johnny gently pulls down her surgical mask to reveal how pretty she really is. Her face, however beautiful, is stonily resigned to what she must do. He looks her perfect nude body up and down again, connecting the slim runway of groomed hair at the top of her vagina, flat waist, and perky young breasts to the pouty rose lips and dark brown eyes that feel like they are burning a hole through his chest. *I'll bet Sully named her right...Sweet Pussy*, he thinks, wanting to prove it for himself. Johnny Brown is the picture of controlled excitement. He feels a nervousness he hasn't experienced with any female for a long time. Slowly and gently, with barely quivering bare fingers, as he's foregone the medical gloves he usually wears for this task, he begins to search her for hidden drugs, giving her orders that she obeys. He touches her slightly at every opportunity; skin more soft and youthfully supple than it even appeared to him when she stood away from him in the doorway; a league apart from the mushy padding on most of the other females. Her face remains emotionless. His breathing quickens as he has her ruffle her hair...bend her head to let him see behind her ears...in her mouth. He inserts a forefinger into her mouth to pull her cheek away from her teeth, hoping she'll close her lips on it to signal a willingness to play, but she doesn't. Instead of disappointment, Johnny's excitement rises; her corruption to be more satisfying than the common compliance he would normally have gotten from his other employees.

"Lift your tongue...now your arms...tits...great," he says, using the last word not to just include his satisfaction with her compliance but his excitement at inspecting every part of her flesh, close enough that he could count her pores if he wanted to and able to pick up the scents of the different planes and crevices of her body. "Now your hands...," he continues, "turn'em over...good, now turn around...lift your feet so I can see underneath."

Johnny stands her in front of a full-length mirror, so he can keep his eyes on her face and frontal beauty while inspecting her from behind. He lays a hand on her shoulder, luxuriates in her shudder, and guides her to slowly bend over, running his hand down her spine and feeling each bump of bone as she complies. The intimacy of feeling something inside her body is exhilarating. Her expression is that of a zombie.

"Alright," Johnny says, "now you gotta bend over an' spread'em for me, so I can see that you ain't hiding nothing inside." When she complies, bending over and spreading her ass with her hands to expose her rectum and open vagina, Johnny gasps. Barely able to control his excited breathing, he slides his hand down and into the dampness between her legs. He then takes a small vial from his pockets, pours the tiniest bit of white powdered cocaine onto his finger wet from her vagina, steadies himself with one hand at the top of her ass, and slides the finger with the drug into her rectum, where it will surge through her body faster than from any other opening.

"I think you an' me are gonna get along just fine," Johnny tells her, barely above a whisper.

9

At Don Filippo's apartment, one floor above his social club, Larry, Nicole, the don, and his wife Mimi, a tough-looking, tough-talking old broad with bleached-blonde hair and too-thick makeup finish up a large Chinese takeout restaurant meal. Mimi immediately lights a cigarette and takes a deep draw of its nicotine.

"Can't you wait till all of us finish?" the don asks.

Mimi ignores him, but only stares at Larry. The cigarette dangles straight down from her too-red lips messed up by the food.

Larry notices her stare. "What? Sparerib stuck in my teeth?"

"Aaii, if I was thirty years younger, you'd see what would be stuck in your teeth," Mimi answers quickly. She turns to Nicole. "Ain't he a handsome sonofabitch?"

"I...uh, uh..."

Don Filippo tells Nicole, "You gotta ignore her."

"Ignore my ass," Mimi says. "It's nice to have a young stud around the house, instead of just an old fart like you."

Larry chuckles, used to the goings on between the two; a ball-breaking full of love accumulated over a half century of marriage. For all the bickering, Don Filippo was known as one of the few mobsters who never had a *commara,* or girlfriend. He'd said his hands were full with his wife, and the thought of having another one was too frightening. The truth was, everyone knew, that Filippo and Mimi were one hundred percent committed to each other and no one else.

Don Filippo snaps back at his wife, "Shaddap! You talk like a goddamn fish woman!"

"Tell me to shut up again, you old fuck," she responds, "and you'll see the undertaker before you get laid again." She turns to Nicole, "Not that he does it so much anymore…even with the fuckin' Viagra."

"Could you believe how I lived with her so many years?" the don says. "God's gotta be givin' me two days credit *up there* for every one I been married."

"Go on. Your luckiest day was when you met me…an' you know it."

Larry laughs, happy to enjoy the affectionate sideshow he hasn't experienced for nine long years.

On the other hand, Nicole is totally puzzled by the relationship, unsure how much of their banter is truly meant but disguised in snappy retorts seemingly designed to entertain. She's never been exposed to that kind of openness around others. Her family, though in a neighborhood similar and not far away, never had much of a family social life. Her parents were only children and carried on their bare minimum tradition by designating their daughter to the same fate. Unlike Larry, who appears amused, the old couple's back and forth only confuses her.

The don turns to Larry. "You need cash?"

"Do I ever."

"Mimi, give him the thing I gave you to hold."

The don's wife goes to a cookie jar in the shape of a pig with a chef's hat, removes a thick manila envelope, and brings it to Larry, who weighs it by bouncing it in his hand.

"Heavy," Larry says.

The don replies, "It's all the money you left with me."

"But the appeals? My commissary?" Larry notices Nicole taking in their conversation, her eyes wide at the sight of the thick packet of cash. "C'mon," he tells Don Filippo, "let's go in the bedroom before she tries to lock us both up for taxes or something." The men get up to leave.

"Just remember who it was that got you *out*, not *in*," Nicole snaps at him, then, under her breath as the don and Larry go to the bedroom, "Jerk." She sits there, steaming as they leave.

Mimi smiles at her in amusement. "Men," she says. "They're all the same. You just gotta screw their brains out, take their money, and ignore them the rest of the time."

"The last part makes sense," Nicole replies.

Mimi only smiles.

* * * *

Don Filippo's bedroom is as ornate as the Vatican, with red and gold velvet fabric and religious dolls and icons everywhere. The don makes himself comfortable on the bed, his back against a bolster on top of the bedspread like a sultan. Larry sits next to him at the edge; neither man willing to mess up the bed cover.

"You know I can't stop all the shit that's going on out in the street," Larry says. "I ain't a fuckin' cop."

"You think I pushed this deal for you to come out an' be a cop?"

"Well, yeah...no, but..."

"But nothing," Don Filippo says. "I got you out to do one thing: prove you wasn't guilty, so that you could be free, with no parole, nothing. What's left of us need you...for *this thing of ours* to live again."

"I can't go back to the old life no more." Larry shrugs his shoulders sadly. "Our thing's all over with...it breaks my heart, but it is. Besides, even if I could get out from under the parole time I owe, I'd wanna get the fuck out of this city for good.

Don Filippo smiles. "Maybe."

"No maybe. Yes. I'm getting the fuck outta here."

"Eh, we see later," Don Filippo says. "Right now you gotta give them a little peace in the neighborhood to buy time." He goes on to advise Larry to push out some Jamaican drug dealers who operate a couple of blocks north of where the social club is located. He points out that there are a few "ball-breakers" down the street on the other side of the club.

"You could do that," the don says. "It won't be hard with your crew. Just give us a little civilized space, like the old days. You made a good start already with those *stroonzi* next door."

"Yeah, if the cops don't pinch us on a complaint tomorrow."

"Cops don't even come here no more," Don Filippo says.

Larry thinks about it then replies, "I guess tonight did feel kinda good."

"There, see? You gonna do it. Just for awhile...just enough to accomplish what you gotta do for yourself."

"I hope so," Larry says. Nine long years have passed since his trial. Even though he knows he was innocent and that reports were faked, he has no idea even how to begin finding a trail to the truth, and he tells that to the old don.

"Don't worry," Don Filippo says. "I'm already reachin' out for that lyin' stoolpigeon, Googi, who testified you was part of that drug deal. His sister-in-law loves me, an' knows we would never hurt him once I give my word."

"Let me know where that motherfucker is, an' I'll make him tell the truth...even if I gotta drag him in by his balls."

"That's what I'm afraid of," the don says. "I'm getting' used to the quiet life."

Both men laugh.

"Relax. I'm in your corner, an' the girl in there, she's gonna help you."

"In a pig's ass," Larry replies. He has about as much faith in Nicole to do the right thing for him as he has for his dead father to come back and play pinochle with him.

Don Filippo laughs at him with amusement, like he would at a cute child, then tosses Larry a set of keys. "Here," the don says, "we even got you set up with a place down the block where youse could all live together."

* * * *

Larry and his men step off a freight elevator into a huge loft that was a garment factory owned by their crew before Larry went to prison. The cutting and sewing equipment, from large wooden tables that cutters laid their patterns on to sewing machines, had all been removed. What remained were interior plaster walls in a sickly green, stained wood plank floors with holes where machines had been screwed to them, discolored pressed tin ceiling that used to be white. The bright spot was that the place had been thoroughly cleaned so there was no surface dirt, and four new queen-sized mattresses still wrapped in clear plastic and a pile of new bedding in burgundies and blues; man colors that wouldn't be allowed in prison...no blacks, blues, or oranges; colors used by regular staff and swat teams. Larry and the men appreciated the consideration, but were still shocked by the bare living quarters. Upon inspection, they found a clean usable bathroom and a kitchen with a refrigerator stocked with ham, cheese, mortadella and other Italian cold cuts. Shelves sported fresh ciabatta bread, dry spices, olive oil, and red wine vinegar. A case of Chianti and one of Pinot Grigio stood side by side on the countertop.

J.B. finishes his tour of their new digs. "It just needs a little work," he says, trying not to be negative.

"I think we'd be better off calling the hotel we just left upstate," Trickster chimes in, "see if maybe they'll take us back."

Boom Boom slaps Trickster on the back of the head. "Don't even joke about that, you little prick," he says, then warns, "You say it, an' it'll happen."

"Sleep with one eye open tonight," Trickster responds as he steps out of Boom Boom's reach.

*   *   *   *

At the same time Larry and his men settle into their new factory warehouse quarters, on a street not far from them young gang members, one side with red garments and one with blue, face off for a battle. The melee begins with knives and pipes, slashing and bashing till blood spurts on others. Soon guns are pulled and shots are fired, causing many to scatter to safety while they are being shot at. Two youths are hit in the back, a few more in non-vital areas like arms, legs, and in one ass cheek. One of the shots crashes through the glass of a barred window then shatters a lamp that rains down shards over a sleeping old couple.

*   *   *   *

Also simultaneously, Johnny Brown stands naked in his private bedroom of his drug factory, with a cellular phone to his ear. Rachel is also naked, but is on the bathroom floor, vomiting into the toilet bowl. After waiting for awhile with no one answering, Johnny angrily slams the phone shut.

10

Nicole enters her building with her pepper spray and stun gun in hand. She cautiously checks out the elevator when it comes, then gets in. At her floor, she looks around carefully then puts the stun gun away in favor of her keys. She opens the door and steps inside, immediately locks the door and drops her pepper spray into her bag. With all the tension seemingly drained from her, she turns toward the apartment, only to be confronted by a male figure coming out of the shadows. Nicole lets out a loud shriek as she fumbles with her bag, trying to retrieve her spray and stun gun, when the light goes on to reveal the intruder as Edward Marshall. Nicole angrily flings the can of pepper spray at him, but misses when he ducks.

"You stupid bastard!" she screams. "You scared the shit out of me!" She flings her entire bag at him. He ducks again, laughing.

"I figured I'd catch you in the act if you were bringing anyone home... you know, "blowing" a mob assignment."

"Don't you fucking dare! You—"

"Whoa, calm down," Marshall says. "I was only joking."

"Some fucking joke!"

"You are getting all bent out of shape over nothing."

"Nothing," Nicole charges, "is not sneaking into my

apartment when I'm out."

Edward Marshall reminds Nicole that he was only able to enter the apartment because she had given him a key. That can hardly be classified as sneaking, he tells her, defending himself in much the way he defends his positions in court. He pours a glass of whiskey from an open bottle that he had already drunk from before Nicole came home.

"Want one?" he asks. "It will relax you.

"If you didn't drag me into the middle of this whole fucking mess," she reminds him, "I would be relaxed. You have no idea what fucking maniacs they are."

Marshall claims that if he had known where it would lead he never would have allowed himself to go along with the Mayor and get involved.

"And me."

"Of course, and you."

He claims that, as disgusting as it seemed to him at the time, he thought it would never amount to more than some back and forth dialogue with the old man, Alessi. Taking Larry Bellino, who he'd worked so hard to incarcerate, out of prison was the furthest thing from his mind. He apologizes to Nicole for underestimating her ability to actually carry out the mission.

"So you sent me there to fail?"

"It would have been better for us all around," Marshall says.

Bad enough Ed had used her because of her being Italian, but he also had done it because he had little faith in her ability; was sure she'd fail at the mission. He'd totally diminished who she was and disrespected everything she'd worked for. *Must have laughed his ass off on his way to Hawaii*, she thinks. *Bastard!* Nicole feels like kicking him in the balls.

"Bellino claims he was innocent," she says, watching Ed Marshall closely to see his reaction.

"He's full of shit!"

"Isn't it possible?" Though Nicole enjoys the irritating effect her defense of Larry Bellino is having on Edward Marshall, she takes note of the fact that he looks away from her as he speaks. "...After all," she continues, "you could have made a mistake."

"I don't make mistakes," he snaps, still looking away. "The only mistake I made is getting involved in this lunacy from the beginning."

"You could have dropped it."

Marshall tells her that he almost did, until he realized he was dealing with an idiot of a Mayor above him who would not give up his plan, even if he, Ed Marshall, refused to participate. "I couldn't give up control."

"So, now you have it," she states with obvious sarcasm. "Are you any happier?"

Ed Marshall gulps down the drink, pours another, then turns to her and forces a smile. He suggests they close the subject for the evening. He tells her that everything will look better...much better for both of them when they wake up in the morning.

"Oh, you're spending the night?"

"Don't you want me to?"

Nicole hesitates. What she would really want, she tells herself, is to throw him out on his ass. However, feeling beaten up and in need for some kind of human to human contact, she says, "Let me go put my diaphragm in."

* * * *

Nicole and Edward engage in sex in her bed. Marshall is on top of Nicole, in the missionary position he prefers; another sign, she believes, of his innate desire for control. He is active and intense, having gone from working his tongue between her legs with no reaction from her other than to pull his head away from her irritated flesh after a time, to sweating and breathing heavily as he pumps his semen into her. Nicole continues to feel detached and unable to participate actively to try for her own pleasure, even when he's finished his climax and collapses next to her.

"That was great, huh?" Marshall asks, huffing and puffing.

Nicole turns over, back to him, and pulls his arm over her. "Just hold me," she says then snuggles against him and closes her eyes.

11

In the warehouse loft that the guys have converted into living quarters, Boom Boom, J.C., and Trickster sleep soundly on three of the mattresses that Don Filippo had provided. One remains empty. Troubled and in his underwear, Larry sits on the windowsill, looking up and down the block at the ruins of his neighborhood. Even though the hookers, pimps, and drug dealers are, as he views it, temporarily gone, it is still decrepit. Larry remembers the past vibrancy of the area; of growing up among family and friends who rallied to support any one of them who had been kicked in the ass by life; of small shops hawking Italian meat and grocery items, ice cream and ices, even a knitting shop. His face reflects his anguish at seeing what the neighborhood's become exactly as his heart and mind feel inside.

J.C. gets up and stumbles to the bathroom, where he takes a leak then shuffles back into the room. He spots Larry and goes to him, taking a spot where he can look out at the street too. "You okay?" he asks.

"I haven't been for nine years, why start now?"

"C'mon," J.C. says, "you weren't like this, even in the can."

Larry continues to stare out onto the desolate shell of the street he grew up on. "I used to play in front of Ciangalini's Bakery," he says, "there, where it looks like it's been bombed."

"And I didn't?"

"Remember old man Ciangialini?" Larry asks. "How he used to bring out those little three-color cookies for us kids, when we looked like we were getting a little wild?"

J.C. pats his stomach. "I used to get big *sfogliatelli*."

Larry goes on as if he's talking to himself. "He never yelled at us, or tried to chase us away from the front of his place. Just calmed us down with food."

"Works for me every time."

Larry finally turns to J.C. "I miss that."

"So do all of us, but you can't go back in time, bud."

"I don't mean go back and be a kid, I know that," Larry replies. "I mean I miss that flavor, that community, that life we had; our pals, the regular people who lived here." He sighs and adds, "I miss it for the kids you and I don't have." He's gripped by images of a time when he came close to being a dad; images of a bloody sheet, a nighttime race to the hospital, the news of a miscarriage just days after he'd been arrested on trumped up charges.

"I understand," J.C. says. "But things change. We change. Maybe we can change this shit back to something good...maybe not exactly the same as it was, but good."

"I doubt it. I guess you're right," Larry admits. "It's like an old romance...you just can't go back."

J.C. takes a more optimistic tone, "Hey, who knows how the future twists and turns? Let's just roll with the punches and see what happens. Go on, get some sleep..." J.C. goes back to his mattress, and to sleep.

Larry continues to stare out at the deserted street. He forces himself to discard all thoughts of the past and turns to the future, thoughts about what he has to do, both for his promise to Don Filippo and to clear his name, and wondering how it will all end. Exhausted, he finally makes his way to the mattress, telling himself that tomorrow is another day; another day to worry about what the first shoe to drop on them will be. *Fuck it,* he thinks, *tomorrow really is another day.*

* * * *

As light begins to flood across the old wood and brick of the warehouse where Larry and his men sleep on mattresses, there is a loud boom downstairs and within seconds SWAT Team members swarm over them. The men, as is the custom for organized crime figures, put up no resistance other than sleepy confusion and are rounded up quickly, cuffed behind their backs, and led out into a police van.

When they reach Philadelphia's Detention Center on State Road, they are thrown into a large holding tank with other criminal-types, from carjackers to rapists.

Boom Boom grumbles to Trickster as they enter. "I told you you'd jinx us, you little motherfucker."

A large black detainee steps up to the men. "Gimme a cigarette." Without a word, Boom Boom hits him a short shot under the chin that drops him to the cement floor like a heap of hookers' clothes. Everyone else steps away from them now. Larry turns to look out miserably from between bars.

"Aaii, here we go again," J.C. says.

"What a shitty furlough," Trickster chimes in. "We didn't even get laid."

"I'll buy you your own fag when we get back upstate," J.C. tells him.

"Both of youse, shut the fuck up before I kill one of youse," Boom Boom orders. "I don't wanna have to listen to this bullshit for another six years."

* * * *

Nicole enters her office feeling dragged out after a miserable night of tossing and turning and wanting to shove Ed Marshall off the bed; one of those nights that often troubled her with elements of a case about to come to court, but with no singular topic beating in her brain. There were just too many implications of what she was involved in for her to focus on any one. The office phone rings as she nears her desk. "Oh God, not even a coffee break," she mutters to herself as she picks it up. The blood drains from her as she's told about the raid on the guys' warehouse digs.

Fifteen minutes later, bursting with contained anger, Nicole enters the chambers of Judge Cleary, whom she had interned for what seemed to her like decades ago. A half-hour later, she's in Judge Cleary's courtroom, watching a balding attorney present a motion to him over the bench.

* * * *

As dusk approaches, Larry and his men are released through the front door of the detention center. Nicole is waiting. She is stiff and angry.

"Aaii, Mother Theresa!" Trickster shouts. He kisses her cheek before she can stop him, but immediately shakes him off and steps away from him when she realizes it.

J.C. hurries over to a hot dog vendor. "Gimme a bunch of hot dogs."

"How many?" the vendor asks, obviously tired after a long day on his feet dealing with the quirks of patrons.

J.C. responds, "How many's in a bunch?" He tells the vendor, "Make believe they're fuckin' bananas," then turns to the others. "Hey, youse want any?"

"Yeah, me, Daddy," Trickster says. He playfully skips over to J.C. Boom Boom, dour as usual, hangs around alongside Larry, who just stares at Nicole.

"Thanks," Larry says.

Nicole hands him a business card. "Don't thank me. Just pay this attorney for filing the writ. Five hundred dollars is what he charged."

"That's cheap. What happened?" he asks.

"God goofed and invented men, that's what!" With that, she turns and walks off.

Larry shakes his head. "I'll never fuckin' understand women."

12

Nicole couldn't wait till Edward Marshall reached her apartment so she could rip him a new ass. To her surprise, he was just as angry as she when he arrived. From that moment till the point they are at, it's been nothing but a continuous screaming match.

"How dare you go against my decision?! Marshall yells.

"How dare you treat me like a fucking child?!" she responds. She feels like hitting him with something, and looks around her immediate area as she continues shouting. "You only let me know what you were doing *after* the arrests! And, you prick, that's after spending the night with me!"

"I didn't want to upset your evening," he says, trying to sound considerate.

"No, you didn't want to go without getting laid!" she responds angrily. "Or, you didn't trust me enough?"

Edward Marshall softens his stance, "Okay, I admit, it was stupid of me. I guess I'm better at public relations than personal relationships," he continues. "I honestly did not want to ruin your night...yours, not mine."

Nicole looks askance at him, softening, but not really sure whether or not to believe him, as he goes on, "Believe it or not, Nicole, although I do not always know how to show it, I really do care about you."

Nicole deflates as her anger ebbs. "For the life of me," she mutters. "I'll never understand men."

13

After hours of working on a plan to clean up their area, Larry and his crew are ready to make their first serious foray into the streets. He had tried to get input from Nicole as to areas hit worst by chaotic crime and where she would like them to start, but she refused to participate, saying the less she knew about what they did the better.

Having pumped themselves up for a task they might like, getting their shit off after years of confinement, and subjugating real worry about the consequences if they're being played by Nicole and her bosses, they move along the street that looks like it hasn't been cleaned since they were incarcerated with a confidence that dares onlookers to mess with them. The men walk in a diamond-shaped formation, with Larry in front, Boom Boom and J.C. on either flank a step or two behind Larry, and Trickster, who keeps turning around to make sure no one threatening is coming up behind them, bringing up the rear.

Many of those who still reside on the block look out their windows above stores that are closed and gated up. Small groups of young black, Hispanic, and white toughs hang out in different spots on the street. Among the others, and in Larry's path, are six rough-looking young white punks who range from late teens to mid-twenties and are abusing a tired-looking woman returning from a store with two bags of groceries. A four or five year old child clings to the woman's leg. Larry stops right at the commotion. The group of punks is distracted enough by the arrival of Larry and his men to let the woman and child hurry away.

"You know," Larry says, "real toughguys don't pick on women and children. They pick on guys like me."

The leader holds his ground, looking Larry square in the eye. "You're that Bellino guy, Mafioso motherfucker, right?"

"Funny, I don't understand a word you said. Maybe it's because you should be in school, learning English."

"You understand this? I hear you're a big time snitch mother—"

Before the words are even out of the punk's mouth, Larry's knee jammed up in the leader's crotch lifts him off his feet, where he then grabs him by the throat and slams him against a lamppost. One toothless punk pulls a knife. Boom Boom moves like lightning to disarm him then cracks his wrist. The sound of the snap and scream startles one of the gang who runs off. J.C. slams two of the punks' heads together and drops them to the ground. Trickster goes into a karate stance, scaring away the remaining punk.

The entire operation takes a couple of seconds. The toothless punk with the broken wrist moans and cries, "My wrist! Oow! Shit, it's broken!" He continues, "Oh fuck, you broke my fuckin' arm! SHIT!!"

Larry tells the leader, "You ever dare to even think the word snitch in the same thought with me, and I'll cut your heart out myself." He tightens his grip on the leader's throat. "You understand, scumbag?" He turns to the crowd. "And that goes for any of you!"

"Shit! My fuckin' arm is broke!" the toothless punk goes on.

"And there's a new rule around here," Larry warns. "I

catch you with a weapon pointed at anybody I know, you lose the hand, just like in a fucking Muslim country. This is now Bellino country. Capisce?" He tosses the leader down onto the ground. "Now don't let me see you or your jack-o-lantern friend on my block again. Get out!"

Boom Boom kicks Toothless as he starts to run away. Trickster goes into an exaggerated karate stance and makes bird-like calls.

Larry turns his attention to the few young white and Hispanic toughs remaining, who did not move throughout the altercation. "You too. Get the fuck outta here!"

None of the youths move. They look to one good looking Hispanic. "Where we supposed to go, man?"

"Anywhere but here."

The young Hispanic waves his arm over the block of boarded up stores. "Should we go hang out in the movie theater?" he asks. "Or the Burger King? Or maybe the bowling alley?"

Larry looks around. All he sees is bleakness and despair in the shuttered buildings and stores. He is at a loss for an answer. "Maybe open one of them up."

"With all our extra cash?"

"That ain't my problem," Larry says, exasperated. "Just go."

"Listen, man, I don't mean no disrespect," the young man says, "but the cops try to chase us, the other gangs try to chase us...now you. Sorry, but we ain't fuckin' moving no more."

Larry scans the lost looks on the youths' faces then surveys the dilapidated neighborhood again. His frustration is apparent. "What's your name?" he asks.

"Pepe...Pepe Garcia."

"Okay, Pepe, don't ever let me hear that you bother anybody around here." Glumly, Larry walks off, with his men following.

Trickster says, "Boy, you guys are sure lucky youse had me along."

"Shut the fuck up," Boom Boom tells him.

Trickster quickly replies, "Please, Boom, don't be afraid to say what's on your mind."

"Boom, just ignore this little flea," J.C. advises.

As Larry steps off the curb, a midnight blue BMW comes to a screeching halt in front of him, blocking his path. The side windows are dark. Larry's men assume fighting stances. A door opens and Johnny Brown gets out, with Sully following him. The driver, Johnny's brother, Carmine, remains in the car. After a prolonged hard stare from Larry and Johnny Brown, the latter opens his arms wide and, smiling, goes to hug Larry.

"Jesus Christ, I don't believe it," Johnny says. "Larry, how the fuck you been? It's so good to see you out. Larry accepts the welcome without responding to the hugs and kisses. He is surface friendly, but trying to make it obvious that he can't stand Johnny Brown without saying it outright.

"I'm okay," Larry answers, "unless you know something I don't."

"Hey, Larry, what the fuck is that supposed to mean?"

"Like maybe you seen my doctor."

"Oh...oh, like that's a joke," Johnny says. "Oh, now I see."

Larry remains silent but smiles inwardly. Johnny Brown is too well versed in mob ways not to pick up the double meaning of Larry's words. *Fuck you where you breathe*, Larry thinks.

"Yeah, that's funny," Johnny goes on with enough of a bitter edge for Larry to pick up. "Like I seen your doctor. I'll have to remember that one."

"Always glad to help you out."

Johnny waves to Boom Boom and J.C. "Hey, how you guys doin'?"

Boom Boom and J.C. nod or return limp waves. There's no doubt that they dislike him as much as Larry does. Trickster steps forward with a hand extended toward Johnny Brown. Hey, Johnny, long time, no see," he says.

"Whoa, what do I look, stupid?" Johnny says. "You got a buzzer in that hand?"

"Would I do that to you?"

"You already did, you little fuck. That's why I ain't shakin' your hand."

Trickster tells him that he's really matured since they last met, and that it was too bad Johnny wasn't with them in prison to witness his maturation process first hand. Johnny smiles tersely. He turns to Larry.

"Speakin' of jail," Johnny says. "I thought you guys had another five or six to go. What happened?"

"We got a 2255 hearing."

Their conversation continues to be tense and full of double meanings. Johnny Brown says Larry's connections must be strong for them to get bail, which organized crime figures almost never get. His meaning that they must have rolled over for the state or feds is not lost on Larry. He adds, "You must have connections I don't know about."

"Like Trickster said, if you woulda spent more time with us these last nine years, you would know more about everything."

"I guess all of us got a lot to learn," Johnny says tersely. He suddenly takes on an uplifted demeanor. "But why talk philosophy. I came looking for you to give you this." He reaches into his inside pocket, which makes Larry and his men tense. Larry prepares to tackle Johnny if he pulls a gun, but all he brings out is an envelope. He smiles, as if aware of their thoughts, and flips the envelope to Larry.

"A little coming home present," Johnny Brown says, "...even though it might be temporary...you know, with the appeal an' all. You know how chancy that could be."

Larry holds out the envelope to return it. "We appreciate it, but, nah, we're okay. We don't need money."

Johnny says, "No, please, Larry, don't insult me. I want youse to have it."

Larry decides not to push the confrontation any further at the moment and tosses the envelope to J.C., who puts it in his pocket. He thanks Johnny and grimaces when Johnny grabs him and hugs him again. He stays still rather than return the hug, which he knows Johnny will understand and not mistake for any chance of them ever being friends.

"Let me know if there's anything else I could do," Johnny says before departing. He ignores the other men, as they do him and his bodyguard, Sully.

"I'm sure you done more than your share already. But maybe we'll see each other soon," Larry replies, leaving the implied threat to hang in the air.

"Yeah, talk over old times," Johnny says with a forced smile that borders on a sneer.

"No, more like new times. Where do I find you?"

Johnny Brown implies a threat of his own, "Don't worry, I'll find you."

* * * *

As Carmine drives away from the confrontation, Johnny Brown speaks on his cellular phone. "Yeah, I just left him," he tells the person on the other end, "an' I'm telling you now, either you do something about him, or I will!" He slams the phone shut and angrily looks out the window.

14

The warehouse loft the guys occupy is in the middle of renovation. Frames have been constructed by a crew of workmen to divide parts of it into separate bedrooms. Dust is everywhere the men work, highlighted by rays of sunlight that appear thick enough to climb. Noise from saws and hammers is deafening, yet none of the guys seem bothered by it. In the main area, as far away from the dust as possible, a makeshift work table is covered with a spread of Italian cold cuts, bread, wine, and condiments like roasted peppers, pickled vegetables, and black wrinkled olives all laid out on white deli wrapping paper with clear plastic wrap over the top of the food.

Nicole finishes filling out official forms then jots some notes on a separate paper. "Well, that takes care of your probation reports for the week," she says.

"You sure you don't want nothing?" J.C. asks her. "The mozzarella knots are out of this world."

"No thank you."

"How about a sopresata and roasted peppers?"

"Whoa, J.C., you only got Italian stuff," Larry says. "You didn't get her no American cheese on Wonder Bread or spaghetti with ketchup."

"Stop being an ass," she replies.

"I'm an ass? I don't hate everything about my own people."

"You are in no way, shape, or form *my* people."

Trickster interjects, "That makes me feel *so* unwanted."

"Hey, we were wanted for a long time," J.C. says, "...by the FBI.

"That's because our last names end in vowels," Larry says.

Trickster adds, "FBI: Forever Bothering Italians."

"Don't insult my intelligence with that bullshit rhetoric," Nicole snaps. She has heard that kind of talk from when she was a teenager, out and about in a neighborhood infested with wiseguys and wannabes. She wasn't sure of it then, but became totally convinced once she got out that the slogans just covered up a darker side of her Italian culture.

"Who should we target," she asked, "Lithuanians? How many of them have you given *buttons* to lately, smart guy?"

Trickster looks down at the fly of his pants. "I got snaps."

"I think I got a zipper," J.C. went along.

"Pass me the cherry peppers," Boom Boom said.

Obviously irritated, Larry tells Nicole that her problem is that she's so ashamed of what she is that she'll eagerly accept the bad about her people, but can't see the good; that because of her attitude she'll believe any line of shit the government hands her.

"No, I'll believe you, a convicted drug dealer."

Larry slams an angry fist on the table. Platters dance from

one side to the other; bottle of Chianti falls over. "I told you I was fuckin' innocent!" he shouts. "An' when I get what I need and prove it, Miss *I Wanna Be Part Of The Brady Bunch*, you're gonna eat those words."

"As long as she eats something," J.C. says, trying to ease the tension. "She's starting to look like a bag of bones."

"I've had enough of this bullshit!" Nicole says. She quickly packs her pad into her bag and stands to leave. Trickster jumps from his seat to help her with her coat. As she walks away, a note Trickster has stuck on the back of her coat reads, "PINCH ME, I'M ITALIAN." The men all stifle laughs. Larry just shakes his head.

While following Nicole with his eyes, J.C. tells Larry in a low voice, "*Marrone a mi*, look at those legs. I wouldn't mind breakin' the headboard with her."

"You'd probably find better action at Graziano's Funeral Parlor," Larry answers.

Nicole stops by the elevator to glare back at them, then gets in and disappears.

Larry tells J.C. to send all the workers home; that he's tired of the noise and he'd rather he and his guys did the rest of the work themselves. Who knows if any one of the workers is a plant and could be sticking a bug somewhere in the loft that would help send them back to prison later on. J.C. pays them and tells them they are not needed anymore. The men look quizzically at each other, but appear too afraid to complain.

Moments after the workers have left, they hear the elevator returning. Larry and his men watch the door cautiously. J.C. and Boom Boom pull pistols from a window sill trap that they open with a pin. When the elevator door opens, Nicole comes in carrying her pepper spray in one hand, and with the other hand is holding Pepe, the street tough, by the collar. He has his eyes covered, and is moaning.

"My eyes! I'm fuckin' blind!" he cries.

"Quick, get me something to get the pepper out of his eyes," Nicole says. She stops when she notices the shocked expression on the men's faces.

"What?!" she says. "He pinched my ass!"

* * * *

Early evening of that same day Larry and his men strut along their street on their way to an important meeting. Through investigation and kicking things around between them, they've decided that this will be the first step on their ladder to completing the assignment none of them likes but each is committed to. As they approach the spot where Pepe and his friends hang out, the youths crowd into a formation that blocks their way. Pepe, pulling Rachel, who works at Johnny Brown's drug factory, and who wears dark glasses, along with him. He lets go of her and moves into the center to confront Larry. The two stare at each other for a moment.

"You okay?" Larry asks.

"Yeah. I was just wondering if what we talked about at your crib is still happening?"

"It'll be taken care of, just like I told you."

"Cool."

Pepe steps back, grabs a reticent Rachel to the forefront, and pulls her forward to introduce her to Larry as his sister.

"Pretty girl." When Larry reaches to touch Rachel's arm as he speaks, she abruptly pulls away. Pepe looks surprised and embarrassed. Larry tries to read her face, but sees only a blank stare; what he always called a *victim's stare*; a stare he'd seen all too often in prison on the faces of those who'd been regularly abused. He adds, "...A little tense too."

Rachel walks off.

"Sorry," Pepe says. "She usually ain't like that."

"It's okay; just keep an eye on her; make sure she's okay. We gotta go.

"Need any help?" Pepe asks.

"No, we got it covered."

"Cool."

Pepe and Larry shake hands, after which Pepe and his boys go back to hanging out while Larry and his men continue walking for a couple of blocks until they come to a gated store with two Jamaicans wearing military jackets and hair in braids standing guard. Reggae rhythms blast out onto the street. Larry steps up to one of the guards and looks him challengingly straight in the eye. He knows from his time in prison that blacks have an innate sense of fear; they can sense who they can fuck with and who they can't. He challenged a bodybuilding Rasta named Morgan after having words with him by having his men stay away from him for a couple of days. The message was *I'm ready, come and see what you think you can do.* He could almost smell the fear in Morgan, who kept his distance from Larry until he was shipped out to another institution.

"Foota here?" Larry asks the lead guard. He almost smiles, knowing that the purpose of the uniforms is to cover the hearts of dogs.

"He be expecting you?"

"You know damn well he is," Larry replies. "Don't fuck with me."

Both Jamaicans laugh, flashing gold teeth as they do. The lead guard says, "Foota say no need to search you, mon. Go'wan in."

Inside, the place is nothing like the kind of social club Don Filippo has. Instead, it's like an unlicensed nightclub. Even at that early evening hour men and women engage in highly sexual dancing, while others drink or smoke pot. Larry figures the place is probably packed after the regular bars close until the early daylight hours. He winces from the smell of marijuana and sweaty sexed up bodies that assault his nostrils. The music feels loud enough to make his ears bleed; every beat pounds in his neck and chest.

"Oooh, dere be de heavy ganga here," Trickster says.

They continue to walk toward the rear. A stunningly beautiful young light-skinned girl in a handkerchief-sized black skirt and a gauzy white blouse that let her nipples peek through blocks Larry's path, dancing seductively before him. He smiles, then steps around her and continues on, fighting the urge to peek back at her over his shoulder. In the back, sitting in the center of a curved leather banquette, he finds FOOTA, a Rasta wearing clothes that resemble a television test pattern.

"Well, well, if it ain't the Mafia mon himself," Foota says. "Sit, Mafia mon, sit. Your boys could put theyselves by the bar; maybe they be getting lucky."

Larry nods an okay for J.C. And Boom Boom to leave then tells Foota, "My nephew sits here with me. He's my *concierge*. Larry's eyes twinkle with amusement at his intentional use of the malapropism. He would have been shocked if Foota had known enough to correct him.

Foota doesn't disappoint him. He says, "Oh, yeah, mon, I seed that in the Godfather movie. Sit, sit. What can Foota do for you?"

"First, I brought you a gift," Larry replies. He nods to Trickster, who fishes a red plastic Italian horn on a gold chain from his pocket. As Trickster leans over Foota's drink to hand him the horn, a stream of powder drops from his sleeve into the drink and instantly disappears.

"It keeps away the evil spirits," Larry says, laughing inwardly at how really stupid people get into positions of power, even in a little pond like their rundown neighborhood.

Foota takes the horn, admires it for a few seconds, turns it over to see all angles then puts it around his neck. "Foota still don't know what it is you want?" he says.

Larry replies without any outward sign of emotion, "Nothing much. You just have to leave this neighborhood. Move somewhere else."

At first, Foota appears confused, trying to make sense of the gift, Larry's quiet demeanor, and an order to leave the area. When it seems to finally register, he howls with laughter then turns deadly serious. "You can go an' fuck yourself, Mafia mon! Foota ain't got no fear of nobody, even Mafia mans. Foota got one hundred guns."

"I don't need guns," Larry says. "I got stronger stuff."

"Like what?"

"Like spirits."

"Spirits?"

Larry points a finger at Foota and warns him to listen and listen carefully for his own good. He tells the Rasta leader that he's got till later that night to close the place and, "...get the fuck out of this neighborhood." Calmly, which he knows can be more frightening, Larry continues, saying that as of the following day there would be no more drug dealing, no more shootouts. He finishes with, "No more showing your ugly fuckin' face here or anywhere near here."

Foota's men move toward Larry, but Foota waves them back.

Larry goes on, "If you ain't shut down and gone by tonight, *mon*, I'm gonna put the worst curse you ever saw on you. You fuck with me and my magic and you're gonna die a slow, painful spirit death."

Though Foota tries to put a front on of being unimpressed, Larry can sense, see in his eyes that the threat has reached the core of him.

"You get the fuck outta here, Mafia mon, while you still could," Foota says. "Foota will be here, in this chair, after you die. Fuck your Mafia spirits!"

Trickster chimes in, "Don't say he didn't warn you."

Larry and Trickster rise to leave.

Larry takes a final stab at Foota, "When the curse starts, don't contact me, or you'll die sooner. Just leave and you'll get better in one day." He makes the sign of the cross at Foota and sympathetically says, "I'll pray for your soul."

As Larry and Trickster walk away, Foota downs his drink then slams the empty glass on the table. Once again, the light-skinned black girl dances in front of Larry, who is flanked by his men. This time he reaches out, touches her face and runs his hand down under her chin, then smiles and steps around her.

"Too bad she won't be around either," Trickster says. "She coulda been my future ex-wife."

* * * *

In a bedroom decorated with beads and bright red, yellow, and green plush fabrics that looks like it was decorated by a Gypsy or a Rajah on LSD, Foota awakens groggily from a drunken sleep. A naked girl sleeps next to him in the bed; her spittle from a drunken slumber stains the red pillow. Foota runs a hand up and down her body, stopping on her ass to fondle the large mounds, smiles, and gets out of bed to stagger to the bathroom. He flips up the toilet seat, leans forward against the wall with one hand, and begins to urinate. The stream of hot urine coming from his flaccid penis is the bright color of blood, thanks to the aqueous soda-based compound that that Trickster dropped into his drink the day before.

The naked girl in the bed is startled out of her sleep by Foota's bloodcurdling screams coming from the bathroom.

*　*　*　*

That night, Larry and his men stroll to the Rasta's club, which is completely locked up and deserted.

*　*　*　*

In the back room of a bar miles from Larry's headquarters in South Philadelphia, members of a biker gang display weapons for sale to three jihadists. The door is suddenly smashed down and SWAT Team police rush in behind shields, guns drawn. One of the motorcycle gang members and two of the jihadists lift their guns to fire, but are shot dead immediately. Everyone else is thrown against the wall and handcuffed.

Outside, Mayor White sits in a car with Ed Marshall. They watch the SWAT Team lead their captives out. The Mayor turns to Marshall, saying, "I don't mind saying I told you so."

The D.A. forces a smile.

*　*　*　*

At the rear table in Don Filippo's social club, Larry and the don sit alongside each other. The young tough, Pepe, sits across from them. Some of the youths from his crowd are mixed in with Don Filippo's old men and Larry's crew; some watch TV while other watch the old men play pinochle and gin rummy, but don't participate. Larry pushes a large pile of banded and stacked money across the table to Pepe

* * * *

On another street, not far outside the South Philadelphia area that used to be Little Italy, where Larry and his men are recapturing their area block by block, police cars pull to a screeching halt between two gangs about to square off with pipes and knives. A gun gets tossed under a car, but the retrieved by a police officer. The cops grab whoever hasn't scattered, and throw them against the wall to frisk them.

* * * *

In an elegant restaurant that is not yet open, Larry meets the well dressed owner. They hug and kiss. The owner pours a glass of dark red Sicilian Nero d'Avola wine for each of them. The two men touch glasses in toast, after which the restaurant owner hands a thick stack of money to Larry, who nods his appreciation.

* * * *

With Larry in the passenger seat, Boom Boom pulls into the parking lot outside the fast food restaurants in a highway rest stop. Both men get out and meet two other men who look like old time wiseguys in black leather jackets and all decked out with gold chains, diamond pinky rings, and other jewelry, and who hand Larry money. They chat cordially for a couple of minutes, hug all around, and leave.

15

In an apartment that might have looked modern and comfortable nearly a century earlier, but has lost any semblance to either, Rachel hands money to her mother, who, like the apartment was once beautiful but has been beaten down by a hard ghetto-style life. Rachel too looks like she is on the same path, appearing noticeably more haggard than just a couple of weeks before. Rachel and Pepe's mother has totally accepted her miserable circumstances; the dilapidated apartment, her four pre-school age children in various shades of brown, reflecting their various fathers, another infant in one arm that sucks at her sagging breast while she reaches for the money from Rachel. She shows no enthusiasm, even for the hope that Rachel tries to instill through money, and two bags of groceries that sit at her feet, and a promise of more to come.

"Mama, please, put this away," Rachel whispers a plea in Spanish. She looks toward a dirty yellow and green floral curtain that serves as a bedroom door. "Hide it...don't let him see it."

"No."

"Promise?"

"*Si*," the woman says, still getting her sagging breast stretched further downward by the sucking infant.

"This will take us back home," Rachel says.

"Yes."

"Palm trees...sunshine...*platinos* growing wild...I'll do whatever it takes to get you there, Mama. I promise."

One of the smaller children comes over and begins rummaging through the bags of groceries for goodies. Rachel catches a bag before it falls, finds chocolate wafer cookies, and gives one to the child. She calls to two of the older ones, Ylses and Paco, to put the rest of the groceries away. They take the bags and hurry of to the kitchen. Rachel's even more frustrated and saddened by how raggedy her siblings look.

"Friday I get some more money, Mama," Rachel says. "I'll buy them some new clothes. Anything special you want?"

Her mom shakes her head slowly and raises her free hand to affectionately pat Rachel's cheek. "You're such a good girl," she says. "Are you working the street?"

"No, Mama, I'm not a hooker. I gotta run now. I gotta be at work." As she kisses her mother's head and starts for the door, she whispers, "Go on, hide it...hide the money."

Rachel's mother takes the money from her lap and stuffs it down into the side of the chair's cushion.

Rachel kisses the children, and wiping tears from her eyes hurries out.

* * * *

As soon as Rachel is gone, her mother's large slimy-looking man of the moment, Juan, comes out from behind the bedroom curtain, and goes directly to the mother of his child, the youngest. He is all spruced up for an outing to a bar, OTB, or wherever the local shiftless and ne'er do wells hang out.

"You got something for me?" Juan asks.

Rachel's mother quickly pulls the money out of the chair, and proudly holds it up for him, the only person or thing that brings her to close to anything resembling life. She waits for the slightest hint of approval from him. With a big, phony-seductive smile, he fondles her face from under her chin, working his hand up until she takes his thumb in her mouth. Full of satisfaction, he leaves the apartment, stuffing the money into his pocket as he goes.

16

Nicole Gianetti and Mimi Alessi come out of a magazine store on the Main, in Philadelphia's surviving trendy area, carrying shopping bags from a number of exclusive stores. Mimi holds a fistful of lottery tickets. A cigarette dangles from her mouth.

"Fuckers wanna break balls about smoking," Mimi complains. "You spend money an' they wanna tell you what to do."

Nicole merely smiles.

Mimi puts down her packages to stuff the lottery tickets into her bag. "Maybe we'll get lucky an' hit the big one," she says. "Remember, we partners."

"That's okay."

"No, it's like a thank you for coming along with me down here shopping today."

Nicole holds up one of the bags she is carrying. "The silk blouse you bought me is more than enough." She adds, "In fact, I wish you hadn't." She means it. One thing Nicole is not used to is receiving gifts. Her parents were frugal that way, insisting that gifts were only commercialization of events. In college her affairs were convenient but not lasting or personal enough for presents. Ed Marshall's biggest gift was to pick up the tab for dinner.

"It's my pleasure," Mimi responds about the blouse. "Wait till you see how good you look in it. Mah, you gonna give more guys hardons."

Nicole's smile quickly becomes a grimace at the coarseness of Mimi's expressions.

"C'mon," Mimi says, "let me take you for lunch."

Mimi and Nicole find an Italian trattoria on North Wayne Avenue, and are seated at a table near the warming glow of a fireplace. A waiter takes their orders. When he walks off to the kitchen, Mimi says, "*Pasta fagioli* my ass. It's *fazoole*. *Pasta fazoole!*"

"Isn't it the same thing, just said a little differently?"

Mimi looks shocked. "Are you kidding?" she says. "They're both beans and macaroni, yeah, but *pasta fagioli* is a few beans in soup. *Pasta fazoole* is like us: thick enough to throw at a wall and dent it, and spicy enough to keep you from forgetting you had it for a long time, no matter what you do."

"Sounds exciting," Nicole replies, thinking it's a dish she can live without.

"How did your mother, or your grandmother, cook it?" Mimi asks.

Nicole was not too high on eating any kind of beans, not wanting to fart as a result, like some of those she'd been around. No burritos; no *pasta fagioli* or *fazoole*. She tells Mimi, "I don't really know how they cooked, or what they cooked. Both of my grandmothers had died before I was really old enough to know them, my mother isn't the best cook in the world…hates to dirty her kitchen," she says, reminiscing. "We ate a lot of salads, tuna fish, and boxed macaroni and cheese…and I sort of grew away from everything else once I entered college."

"Grew away from what?"

"Any ethnic food...Italian food."

"Where'd you go to school, England?" Mimi asks.

"No.   But even here, all the ethnic stuff was...well, different. I wanted to blend. Pizza, maybe a chicken *parmigiano* was the most I'd have. My main meals were peanut butter and jelly or store roasted chicken."

"That'll all change. The older you get, the more you'll wanna connect with your roots, understand where you come from and where you belong, trust me."

"Maybe...I guess," Nicole says.   "I'm not sure I have roots...maybe Chicken of the Sea or Skippy."

"I see I'm gonna have to take you under my wing," Mimi says, "like a grandmother, and teach you about life...our life...*la vita Italiana*."

Nicole asks Mimi if she has any grandchildren, real ones of her own, not adopted ones like Nicole finds herself becoming? That feeling confuses her. For all her coarseness, Nicole senses the kind of warmth and protection that makes her want to cuddle up on the sofa with the woman. On the other hand, she is put off by the thought of Mimi dropping cigarette ash onto her while she's snuggling. Mimi takes photos out of her wallet and shows Nicole. They are of a priest and a nun.

"I don't know what happened; if they loved God or hated us more," Mimi says. "Anyway, he got'em both, and we got no grandkids."

"I don't know what to say."

"There's nothing to say," Mimi says with resignation. "It is what it is."

The waiter arrives with their food, sets it down and walks off. Nicole has a beet salad with a goat cheese purse, candied pecans, and a balsamic-vinaigrette. She begins to dig in while Mimi turns her thin *pasta fagioli* with a spoon.

"See, what did I tell you?" Mimi groans. "Water and beans. You gotta think like us to cook like us."

"I'll remember that."

Mimi goes on complaining. She guarantees Nicole that the cook's a Mexican or from the North of Italy, like Venice or Florence. She takes a sip of the soup, turns up her nose, then looks up at Nicole.

"Did you ever think of going back to your natural dark hair?" Mimi asks. "I'll bet you'd look terrific...like a real guinea."

Nicole is less than thrilled by the compliment. She smiles but shudders inwardly.

*   *   *   *

Back in the neighborhood, J.C.'s gives a lesson to, Tommy, a young member of Pepe's crew.

"You wanna kill people, you use a .38 or a .45," he says in a low, conspiratorial voice. "You point it at their head...and you pull the trigger..." His face begins to redden and his voice gets louder. "...You DON'T kill them with salmonella because you didn't wash your hands after you touched a fuckin' raw chicken!

Capisce?!"

The two stand in the kitchen of an Italian deli being built. Most of the workers are from Pepe's bunch of young men, who scrub used equipment or finish up walls and floors covered with materials that will pass inspection before they open.

"I gotta wash'em with soap, or just water?" Tommy asks.

"No, with shit!" J.C. answers. "After you touch a chicken, you make sure you stick both hands UP YOUR FUCKIN' ASS!" He looks over to see another of the crew workers putting shelves on the floor, and yells, "Hey, you, asshole! I said they go *off* the floor, so we could clean under'em!"

He starts for the door, mumbling to himself, "*Vafancoulo*! Fuckin' idiots! I need a rest." When he gets outside he runs into Larry, who is walking past the storefront arm in arm with Don Filippo. All around them on the block are signs of activity as stores are being refurbished for reopening by Pepe's friends, outside workmen, and Don Filippo's old men supervising. Some neighbors watch, while others chip in with cautious efforts to help.

Hurrying past Larry and the don, J.C. throws his arms up in the air, saying, "I need a fuckin' break...fuckin' kids make me wish I was back in jail."

Larry and the don look after him and laugh. Three adjoining stores are also being worked on by former young toughs; one has the barber pole Larry saw on the closed barber shop he used to frequent before he went to prison. Neighbors watch. Even the old men from Don Filippo's club now mill around outside the gate.

Larry separates himself from the don and enters one of the other stores, where Boom Boom works with youths who look like weightlifters, putting together a workout gym. A delivery man stands alongside a newly-shipped order of equipment. Boom Boom goes to him and puts a muscular arm around his shoulder.

"We got, what, sixty, ninety days to pay?"

"No, my father said to collect for this stuff today."

Boom Boom tightens his grip as he walks the man to the door. "A hundred-an'-twenty days? Gee, tell your old man thanks."

The exercise equipment distributor's son/delivery man struggles to try and extricate himself from Boom Boom's grip. "Whatever you want," he says. "Take a year for all I care." When Boom Boom finally lets him go, he rushes for the open door and with a panicky look on his face, runs past Larry as he enters.

"Everything okay?" Larry asks.

Boom Boom replies as if he didn't just extort the exercise equipment from the delivery man. "No problem at all."

Larry shakes his head, not wanting to know for sure what he suspects, and continues on his way with Don Filippo. As they walk, their conversation resumes about a message the don has received from someone who might be able to convince an old associate of theirs who went bad and testified at Larry's trial, Googi, to supply some information that can help Larry prove his innocence.

"Thank God," Larry says.

"Don't worry, we're gonna set up this meet."

"I wanna be there."

Don Filippo nixes that idea. He says he's worked through

very quiet channels to get to Googi, and is not even sure that the go between has told the stoolpigeon what's happening. When Larry curses Googi and says he'd love to get his hands around his throat for lying about him at trial, the don points out that emotions Larry carries is exactly why he has to lay the groundwork alone to clear him. They know he didn't falsely implicate Larry and his men in a drug deal on his own, and, Don Filippo says, they need to peel the onion carefully to get to the core of what happened; strip away the layers until they discover the rot inside.

Just then, cab pulls up. Nicole and Mimi get out carrying a number of large shopping bags.

"What're youse doing," the don asks, "stocking these here stores from Main Line stores?"

"Yeah, with bloomers and bras," Mimi retorts. "You wanna see'em?"

"No, please, we got enough trouble here," Don Filippo says. "I just hope youse robbed all this stuff. Money's tight."

They all laugh.

Mimi asks which of the stores will be a restaurant. Larry points out the store where J.C. will be running a deli, but says they have no plans for a restaurant any time soon.

"But a good Italian restaurant?" Mimi asks. "One where they make real pasta fazoole?"

Larry shakes his head no, but Mimi persists, "Why don't you open one? Jesus himself knows we need one, an' you'd be great in a restaurant."

"Not me," Larry says. "I'm looking to get as far away from this place as I can. As soon as I show I was framed, and get the parole dropped...I'm outta here."

"Here we go again," Nicole groans.

Larry snaps back, "But, go fuck yourself."

Mimi pulls Nicole away from Larry to diffuse the argument then hurries back to Larry and whispers in his ear not to pay any attention to Nicole; that she's a good girl, but needs to spend more time with her; that she'd teach Nicole how to be the kind of person she believes she's afraid to expose. Don Filippo chimes in, telling Larry that now he's really in trouble; that he's got both women to deal with.

"Waste your time if you want," Larry says, "but as far as I'm concerned, you're just wasting your time and effort." He adds, "She's a lost cause."

Just then, Pepe, Rachel in dark glasses and looking drawn, and Trickster wander over from another store. When Pepe notices Nicole, he raises his hands to his face. You ain't gonna spray me, are you?

"Not as long as you keep your hands off my ass," Nicole says. She points at Trickster and adds, "And stay away from that clown."

Trickster bows. He steps close to Rachel, who has an expression that combines indifference with apprehension. "Do we make a nice couple, or what?" he asks everyone. Rachel shrinks from him. "You could tell she loves me," he says, "by the way she ignores me."

Larry hands Pepe a bundle of cash held together by a thick rubber band. Nicole's eyes open wide at the sight of hundred dollar bills on top of the pile. Her mind starts to tabulate how much there could be in that stack.

"Thanks," Pepe says, sticking the money into an inside pocket of his jacket. The real problem, he tells Larry, is the red tape involved in obtaining a Certificates of Occupancy for the soft ice cream business he and his friends are trying to start. He says the City has so many rules that he doesn't know how he's going to stay open even if he finally launches his business. "I don't want you to blow all this money."

"Don't worry, we ain't blowin' nothing," Larry says. "We're the smart guys, not the ones who run Shakedown City." He shoots a smirk at Nicole, as if she were responsible for all the ills of the city's administration. He turns to his nephew, "Trickster, could you work it out? I don't care how." He looks at Nicole again, daring her to interfere.

"No problem," Trickster says.

Nicole finally chimes in, "This is all wrong. You can't build a house of cards like this."

"Pinochle or rummy?" Trickster asks.

"I'm serious."

"When aren't you?" Larry asks.

Nicole's frustration turns her face flush with pink becoming red. "Are you all stupid?" she asked, wondering for an instant if she was really dealing with incorrigible morons? "You can't work with money out of paper bags and without permits. Everything will collapse around you and everyone else you're trying to help. You need to account for everything." She pauses to look questioningly at Larry, as if the money may be proceeds from illegal activities.

"It's all legal...borrowed from friends," Larry says.

She looks skeptically at him.

"I swear, it's all legit."

"Well, then, you have to show it on paper, so that later on you'll be able to get loans, expand, even sell a successful business. And, you must comply with government regulations, like them or not."

Pepe immediately jumped in. "We can't. They're ridiculous, and way too expensive. I don't know how anyone can open a business in this damn country?"

"Know of a better one you want to live in?" Nicole snaps.

"She's half right," Larry tells Pepe. "We do have to do things right. I'll reach out for an accountant. He'll set you up with books, the bank, everything." He then turns to Trickster. "Get all the permits they need, fast, from you know who, if he's still around."

Nicole walks away, saying, "I don't even want to hear this."

Trickster crosses one arm over a raised fist in an "Italian salute," then turns back to Larry. "I'll take care of it fast, so me an' Rachel can get married." He winks at Rachel, who shudders.

"I was thinking more in our lifetime," Larry says.

*   *   *   *

Trickster sneaks into the Municipal building in the three a.m. darkness. His entry into a back door is accomplished through the use of a ten year old key that the crew's expense fund had paid for before all of them went to prison, just in case they ever had a use for it. Fortunately, the lock had not been changed during the intervening years and that night would justify the decade old cost.

Contrary to his normal comic's demeanor, he is quietly serious as he moves about through the back hallway and up a staircase. Most surprising to him is that the building still has not been outfitted with cameras everywhere beyond the front lobby entrance area and elevator doors on that level. When he gets to the fourth floor, he, Boom Boom, and a third petrified-looking man with glasses, tan Dockers, and a plaid wool jacket slip through the door and slink along the dark hallway that he believes must be just as dingy in the daytime till they reach the City Permits Office. The man with the glasses looks around nervously, as if searching for a way to escape his companions. Boom Boom drags him into the office by his collar. Once inside, they choose one of the computers and sit their "guest" at it. The man, in his computer world element, finally comes alive and begins to busily work till he brings up PERMIT APPLICATIONS on the monitor.

* * * *

Nicole enters the front door of the Municipal Building just seconds after Trickster, Boom Boom, and their computer tech leave through the back door they'd used to sneak in. She signs a book at the night guard's desk.

"How're you doing tonight, Miss Gianetti?" the guard asks. "Awful late for you to be here."

"Just a little paperwork I have to clear up before I go to

court in the morning," she replies.

On her way to the elevator, she hears the guard shout, "I hope you're getting double-time."

"I'd need a union for that," she shouts back as she enters and presses five. She thinks that Larry would probably have a phony union charter he could sign people up with to shake down employers.

She gets off on the fifth floor and goes to a small office with her name on the door. It also states CONSUMER FRAUD DIVISION. At ease from the knowledge that the building is otherwise empty but anxious about what she's about to do, she enters the office, puts down her bag, gathers up two small books then hurries out. At the end of the hall, she opens an exit door to a staircase and uses one of the books as a doorstop before going in and racing up two flights of stairs. She uses the second book to keep the door on the seventh floor open. When her heels click loudly she removes her shoes and cautiously proceeds to a door marked RACKETS DIVISION. She keeps her right hand crossed over her heart, which seems noisier than her heels had been, opens the Racket Squad door with her left, and quickly steps inside.

Nicole's eyes have barely adjusted to the darkness from the more brightly lit hallway, when she makes out a shadow of someone who charges at her and hits her with a shoulder block that sends her head smashing against the doorjamb. As she falls she bangs her cheek on the floor, yellow and orange explode behind her eyes while whoever hit her runs off. With a groan, she rolls over and pulls herself up enough to lean against the wall. She sits there, moaning and clearing her head for awhile, then feels her face for blood. Nicole finds none, but recoils from touching a sore spot. She rolls her head around on her neck, happy that nothing feels broken, then looks up to see the file cabinet open. She struggles up and checks the files, thumbing across names from *Bell, Randy* to *Belmondo, Jose.* She frantically mumbles, "Bellino...Bellino...Bellino...," only to find the Bellino file missing. "Fuck!"

* * * *

An hour later, D.A. Edward Marshall, drink in hand, paces nervously in Nicole's apartment while she applies ice in a zip lock bag to her cheekbone.

"I knew the minute I heard this ridiculous scheme that there would be trouble," Marshall complains. "Bellino had that file taken."

"Could be," she responds. "I know he's capable of it, though I don't know why he would, when he could have – "

"How could you know? The only way to think like them is to be as morally rotten as they are."

"Morally challenged is more politically correct."

"This is no time for humor," the D.A. snaps.

"Edward, I'm tired..."

Marshall presses her, "Are you sure you didn't see who hit you?"

"I told you, there was nothing I could see. It all happened too fast."

"But does Bellino know that?" he asks, and offers to post a

police guard by her door.

Nicole refuses any security. She argues that all she needs is sleep, and asks Marshall to leave.

As he prepares to leave, Ed Marshall warns again that Mafiosi like Bellino can be dangerous. "You, more than anyone should know they can't be trusted," he adds.

Yes, me more than anyone, she thinks, seething. Would she ever be seen as a person instead of an Italian somehow connected in one way or another to all the stereotypes of the Mafia? When Marshall kissed her on the cheek before leaving, she wanted to punch him; to see his nose bleed. He was fast becoming as repulsive to her as Larry Bellino and his thugs; maybe more.

Still smarting from Ed Marshall's words, Nicole looks around the room, at the bareness of the décor that is the antithesis of the cut velvet and bright colors of Mimi Alessi's taste...at the loneliness. Her face burns and throbs at the same time. She goes to the bedroom, angrily drags Ed Marshall's photo from its frame, rips it and tosses the pieces in the trash, then grabs the shopping bag from her day out with Mimi Alessi. She pulls out the gift, a sexy, scoop-necked bodysuit she would never normally wear. She holds it up to her in front of the mirror as tears begin to roll.

* * * *

The next day after work, Nicole makes her way to Don Filippo's apartment above his club. The previous night had been miserable, with sporadic spells of sleep and longer periods of tossing, turning, and struggling to return to unconsciousness while her mind fought against it minute by minute. Her day so far has been just as bad, with a lack of sleep hangover and relentless annoyances at the office. By the afternoon she'd refused to return phone calls, especially Larry Bellino's. After all, she had told herself, the bastard was the cause of all her problems. Finally, needing refuge, she'd punched out an hour early and started for the only place she knew she would find comfort.

While Don Filippo stirs pasta, Mimi sits alongside Nicole, gently pressing a bag of frozen peas to the latter's cheek. She speaks with the cigarette still dangling from her lips, "It's really too late for ice to help...or *piselle*...peas." She adds, "I forget you don't understand Italian."

"I know what peas are. They're freezing my face."

"You want me to take'em away?"

"That's alright, I'm okay," Nicole replies, then adds, "I'm just so goddamned pissed at him."

The don brings the pot to the table and begins plating the linguine with shrimp in a fresh tomato-basil sauce. He says, "Who me? I get you mad? You don't like shrimp?"

Mimi ignores her husband's joke, and answers Nicole directly, "But Larry told you he didn't do it."

She wishes she could have enough faith in one person's word...any person, as Mimi and Don Filippo have in Larry's. "That doesn't mean it's the truth she says," willing to poke a finger in the old couple's eyes; to lash out at anyone. Unlike them, Larry struck her as an abject liar; charming, with a con man's smile and flirty eyes, but a liar nonetheless.

"It has to be," Don Filippo chimes in seriously. "He told me the same thing...and I know Larry would never lie to me." When she looks skeptical, Don Filippo adds, "Unless you think

I'm lying?

"No, I..."

"Leave her alone, already," Mimi scolds the don. "She been through enough without you breakin' her balls." She turned to Nicole, "Go ahead, eat, then you lay down, rest, watch TV. You'll feel better. Maybe you even sleep here for a couple of days, if you want."

Nicole shrugs. The warmth and genuine goodness of Mimi touches her in a way she's not used to. Though she knows she will never take the don's wife up on the offer, she's not about to turn her down at the moment and give up the kind of nurturing she hasn't had since she was a child.

17

In a dark, bucket of blood-type bar that smells like a beer filled urinal mixed with body odor and cigarette smoke, Johnny Brown sits at a rear booth with a stoned-looking Rachel next to him and Sully on her other side. Rachel's halter top is low cut and gaping enough to show maximum cleavage and make it obvious she's got nothing on underneath it. Across from them, three members of the Philly Rogues motorcycle gang can't rip their eyes from Rachel's exposed flesh. The leader speaks to Johnny Brown without tearing his eyes away from the girl's breasts.

"You bring it?"

Johnny nods to Sully, who pulls a bag of drugs from his jacket and tosses it onto the table in front of the grungy-looking leader, forcing him to look away from Rachel for the first time since they all sat down together. He looks at the bag, opens the top, feels and tastes the contents, then nods his satisfaction to Johnny. When the man smiles his front teeth show all silver. Johnny Brown is repulsed by him, but smiles. He gently rubs the back of his fingers along Rachel's cheek, down her neck, and onto her chest. The Rogues' leader's hungry stare at the action amuses Johnny.

"You like this, huh?" he asks the biker.

"What's not to like?"

"Nothing," Johnny replies, "especially in the sack. Her pussy is like a live animal that hasn't been fed in days."

The leader practically drools. "Man, I'd make that pussy purr."

"Problem is I don't share."

"Shit!"

"But I do give things away," Johnny adds. "Do what you're supposed to and she's yours. Consider her a bonus." He dips his hand into her blouse, cradles a breast so that the biker can see it all then tweaks her nipple with his thumb. Rachel groans in her drug stupor.

"Good God!" the biker exclaims, then says to his men, "Let's get going." They all slide out of the booth and hurry off.

* * * *

Building and cleanup activity is at a peak on the block Larry and his men have moved back into. Larry leans against a parked electrician's truck and admires the progress they've all achieved since having been released from prison. Memories of how it used to be, complete with images of his father assuring someone with a problem that he'd take care of everything, Jasper the barber playing operatic arias loud enough for all who passed by his shop to hear, Nonna Lena handing out candy to all the children who'd gather around her when she stepped out onto the stoop…and he smiled. Boom Boom and J.C. drag him out of his reverie with conversations about details he thinks they could have done and left him to his sweet memories.

Suddenly, Pepe hurries to them and without so much as a "hello" or "excuse me," says, "Larry, quick, I gotta talk to you."

* * * *

Mayor White and District Attorney Marshall argue in the Mayor's office as much as an underling can argue with the boss. He claims that taking Larry and his men out of prison was ridiculous at the outset.

"It has gone far enough," Marshall says. "We must put a stop to it now."

"Now?" the Mayor asks, "just when things seem to be getting under control? I am even impressed."

"Was it the burglary at my office that gave you that impression?"

"Don't be condescending. I don't like it?"

"Jonathon, things are not what they appear to be."

"Appearance is everything," Mayor White argued. "I am being honored at a Chamber of Commerce dinner...press, money, voters...my party's chairman." He reminded his district attorney that they were doing what they had to for the greater good, which was to get him into the Governor's Mansion with the power to really get at the root of the state's problems, and to fix them.

"What good will any of it do for us, the state, or the victim when these thugs we have let out onto the streets kill someone?"

"If history tells us anything," The Mayor replied, "it will probably be each other they kill, which is also an improvement." He smiled, "You have to begin looking at the glass as half full."

"I'm serious."

"So am I, Edward," Mayor White answered quickly. "We're down to days until I get that nomination. After that, do whatever you please. Just make sure you do it quietly, and without rocking the boat before the election."

Ed Marshall starts for the door.

"...If you do, Edward, it will be your balls swinging on the mast...alone."

* * * *

Inside the bucket of blood bar where Johnny Brown had his meeting, the Rogue biker leader prepares his troops for battle. They all fortify their courage and enthusiasm with a variety of drugs and booze that they pass around to each other. The air is as celebratory as a primitive group of warriors would conduct before going off to battle. When they've satisfied their pharmaceutical and alcohol desires, they grab shotguns and automatic rifles and shove their way out into the afternoon sunlight.

Outside, they pile into two cars that start down the block. As they near the corner, a garbage truck with a raised snowplow turns into the block and speeds directly toward them. It hits the first car head on, shearing off the roof with the plow as it rolls up onto the vehicle. The group from the second car jumps out with guns drawn and starts firing. Simultaneously, Police SWAT Teams emerge and fire at the Rogues from doorways. Other team members rush into the rogue's bar for a raid. The Rogues are cut down by police fire, but not before one bullet shatters the windshield of the garbage truck as it backs out of the block.

In the garbage truck Boom Boom, bleeding and in pain from a shoulder wound, backs out around the corner and takes off.

18

Larry's block is more alive than ever before, not with tourists, but with neighborhood activity reasonable for that evening hour. A few of Pepe's friends, calm and confident in appearance, stand around in guard-post positions, looking up and down the street. The difference is not lost on Nicole as she gets out of a taxicab and walks toward the building where Larry and his crew live. Her hair has been dyed dark and her makeup has been applied to give her a more glamorous and more ethnic look.

Upstairs, she finds Larry's men along with Pepe and some of his friends drinking and celebrating with sexy females from their late teens to only a few years beyond that. Boom Boom wears no shirt over his heavily bandaged torso. On a sofa, Trickster seems starry-eyed talking to Rachel. They all stop the celebration when they see Nicole, seeming shocked at her appearance. She looks around for Larry, but doesn't see him. Uncomfortable and testy because of the others staring at her, she asks curtly, "Where is he?"

"Upstairs...on the roof," J.C. replies, stammering.

As she starts up the stairs, they look at each other, then burst out laughing and resume their party.

Nicole hesitantly comes through the door onto the roof, not sure what she might find. A cool breeze brushes her hair back. She looks around and to her relief spots Larry looking out pensively onto the street. As she starts toward him, another figure emerges from the shadows and walks in her direction. It is a flashy young blonde in a silky white dress that shows every curve and dip of her body; the hem so high that she could have sex without wrinkling it.

As the blonde hurries past, she snaps, "Good luck with him."

Larry turns his head at the sound. His stony expression changes to a double-take when he sees her.

"I'm sorry," she says. "...I didn't know. I'll go."

"No need. She was leaving anyway." Larry turns back to stare out at the street.

Nicole hesitantly walks to him. "You should be happy," she says. "It would have been a bloodbath, with nothing left on this street. You saved it...you and Rachel...and Pepe the ass pincher, of course."

"Yeah, I'm fuckin' thrilled."

"What's wrong?"

Larry continues to stare out into the night. "Nine years ago, I would have taken care of that situation by myself, in my own way...not with cops an' a SWAT Team."

Nicole wants to tell him what an ass he sounds like, sad that he couldn't shed blood himself, but instead reminds him of the day she picked them up at the prison and drove them back to the barber shop Larry insisted they go to; the one they found closed. "J.C. was right," she adds. "Things do change."

"We grew up with a tradition," Larry says, still staring out over the city and not looking at Nicole. "We took care of our own. My old man did it...so did my grandfather and his grandfather.

Cops were our enemies."

"I know how it must bother you, but..."

"That's the problem, it doesn't. It doesn't, yet it does," he says. "It doesn't bother me that much that I worked with you...the cops...but what bothers me most is that I don't care...that I lost everything I grew up to be...that no matter what I tell everybody else, the time in jail really did take its toll."

"Give yourself credit. Don't confuse smartness with weakness."

When Larry finally turns to face Nicole, his face is full of confusion and pain. He tells her that he feels like all of his years were wasted; that he could have done more with his life... anything...had a house in the suburbs and a bunch of kids by now. It's a side of him she's never seen; a side she's never imagined he was capable of; a side that touches her in a way that confuses her.

"Tomorrow's another day," she says, wishing she had something more profound to add.

With a touching sadness in his eyes, Larry wonders out loud what difference time would make when he doesn't know who he is anymore. He suddenly stops talking to take sharper notice of Nicole. He stares at her hair and makeup; at the sexy top Mimi had bought her showing through her open coat.

Nicole fidgets nervously; she touches her hair then pulls her coat closed. She chuckles self-consciously, and says, "I guess a lot of us don't. I feel stupid."

When she turns to go Larry takes her arm to stop her. "No, it looks good...everything."

"Really?"

"Yeah."

"Don't fuck with me, Bellino."

"No, I mean it," Larry says. "You look more... like, uh..."

"Go on, say it: like a guinea?"

"No...more...real. That's it...real." Larry reaches to touch her hair and runs his hand down toward her shoulder. She bends her head into his touch, then straightens up and shudders.

Misreading the forces that course through her body and brain, Larry asks if she's cold.

"I was."

After staring at each other for a moment, allowing emotion to take over from intellect, Larry moves in to kiss Nicole. She hesitates at first, her head spinning, but finally plunges in with gusto. As if a long kept prisoner is released within her she presses in, wanting to consume into her body the freedom of him; the smell; the taste...to inhale him. She dances with his tongue in her mouth then enters his to run along his teeth and dance some more. Nicole feels otherworldly, her body seeming to separate into one active and one viewing as he lowers her to a padded lounge chair in their roof garden patio set, and begins to undress her. Cloth peeling against her flesh inflames nerve endings. He kisses her neck and shoulders then her breasts, stopping to gently suck and bite each nipple. Flesh burning, she arches her body for him to remove her panties and catches her breath as he mounts and enters her. Full of unfamiliar feelings during any of her previous sexual encounters, she wants her skin to wrap around his entire body and not let him go; wants her blood and organs to meld with his. The two move in slow tandem as if on a toddler's automated ride in a toy store. Heat rises at Nicole's core. Her insides swell until her body cannot hold them anymore. Waves of heat explode inside her, one following the other as he matches her intensity with a flood of his own. They remain locked with him inside her as she slowly deflates.

"You okay?" Larry asks, looking oddly unhappy after his muscles relax.

"Was I that disappointing?" Nicole suddenly feels as if she is not only naked on the outside, but on the inside too.

"No...no, you were fine...you were great." He kisses her forehead, but still appears disturbed.

"A good actor you're not." She pushes him off and reaches onto the floor for her panties.

Larry grabs her hand to stop her. "I told you it's not you. It's just that..."

"What?"

"Just that I've just never been allowed to be happy," he says.

Nicole stares into his eyes, trying to detect some phoniness; some sign of him playing her either because he was horny and anyone would do or because he wanted something more of her, like Ed Marshall always seemed to; or maybe just wanted to abuse her authority and use it as a weapon to blackmail her with tomorrow?

Larry goes on, "Something always happens to fuck it up: jail for something I didn't do...Elena dying. What's waiting around the corner now?" He ruminates that he feels like a torture victim who has water splashed in his face to revive him for more punishment.

Does she feel as though her heart and brain are becoming liquid because she is needy and wants to believe him, she wonders, or is he in as much pain as he appears to be for the first time since she saw him in the prison visiting room? Is she looking at a contrived façade or into his heart? Choosing to believe the latter, Nicole tries to encourage him to think positively. "This is a new life for you."

"That's what I'm afraid of," Larry says. "In my old life, I was more prepared to defend myself and everyone around me." He asks her what would have happened had Pepe's sister not accidentally overheard the rogue bikers planning to attack. "Do you know what could have happened? What could have happened to you?"

"But she *did* hear," Nicole answers. "And, something will always save you, because you are doing a good thing. Just don't worry so much."

"You know, I've still got to get away from here when this is over," he says with stubborn but very little conviction.

"In a pig's ass, Bellino. I just made a major investment in you." Nicole grabs Larry and kisses him passionately again.

*   *   *   *

By the time a post-sex disheveled Nicole enters the loft hand in hand with Larry, the place looks like a party bomb exploded. Clothing and empty liquor bottles decorate floor and furniture. Any sign of humanity has vanished except for Trickster sitting upright on the sofa watching television. He's shocked alert when he sees Nicole and Larry holding hands.

"Do I need to get a tuxedo?"

"For once, don't be a smartass," Larry says.

"I thought I was the only sick puppy here, hung up on a kid like Rachel."

Nicole smiles at him as she lets Larry lead her to his room.

19

The usual activities of building up the neighborhood continue, with some of the new shops about ready to be opened up to the public on Larry's block. The street is livelier and brighter than ever. Larry, with Don Filippo near him, speaks to J.C. and a couple of the workers. Nicole stands next to Larry; closer and more relaxed than ever. Their body language is that of lovers, with her leaning into him and touching him at every opportunity. Further along, Trickster is obviously trying to make points with a haggard-looking Rachel, who wears dark glasses.

From the passenger seat of Carmine's car in the cross street of Larry's block, Johnny Brown takes in the entire scene. Johnny focuses first on Nicole and the body language between her and Larry then scans the block until, after almost missing her because of her different appearance, he spots Rachel with Trickster. Suddenly his entire anger focuses on the girl. He gnashes his teeth angrily.

"So that's how they found out," he says. "Look there, by that scumbag, Trickster. Recognize her?"

"Oh shit," Carmine replies. "Hey, man, a cunt's a cunt."

"Shut up! Let's get the fuck outta here."

* * * *

Later that evening, Carmine drives with Rachel between Johnny Brown and Sully in the back seat. Rachel, who is in a short shimmery-silver nightclub ready dress, is extremely nervous and jittery. She looks fearfully at Johnny and Sully. Carmine drives them through a neighborhood that is solidly skid row. He pulls into an alley where bums sleep huddled in back doorways and against garbage dumpsters.

Suddenly, Sully grabs Rachel and pulls her back onto him, holding her sideways on the seat from behind. She screams and kicks wildly, forcing Johnny back against the other passenger door. Her skirt is up to her hips, her thong urine-soaked and baring every element of her vagina as she kicks. Johnny removes a hypodermic needle from his jacket, then moves forward to pin her bare legs. He pushes the injection into the soft flesh of her inner thigh as she screams. Sully continues to hold her tight and Johnny keeps her legs pinned. Soon her body begins to convulse. Her eyes roll back, her screaming stops…and she dies.

Sully opens the car's door, drags her out, and wedges her next to the filthy wall behind a dumpster. He leaves her there, looking as if she is a hooker sleeping off a bender, then gets back into the car.

Carmine drives off.

* * * *

A couple of hours after Rachel's murder, a fully dressed Don Filippo sleeps sitting up on the bed while his wife sleeps in normal nightclothes under the covers.

At midnight an alarm clock rings on Don Filippo's nightstand. Jarred awake, he quickly shuts it and gets out of bed. Mimi awakens, but is drowsy.

"What's the matter?" she asks.

Don Filippo gives her a gentle pat on the head then stands and stares at her for a wistful moment. "Nothing. I just gotta go downstairs an' meet Larry. I'll be up soon."

* * * *

A half hour later, the don sits alone at his back table in the club. He drums his fingers nervously on the table's brown leather top. His face shows no expression. After what seems like an eternity to him the back door opens and Googi, a four-hundred pound mobster, cautiously enters. Googi looks around, as if he expects to be walking into a trap.

"Thank you Don Filippo, for leaving the door open," Googi says, still looking around nervously. "I wouldn't want to wait outside an extra minute, even at this time of night."

The don asks, "Whose fault is that?"

Googi hangs his head but doesn't answer.

"...But that's why we're here," Don Filippo says, "to fix it, an' make you able to walk these streets again, right, Googi?"

Googi hurriedly sits in a chair near the don. Full of anxiety, he leans in toward him as he speaks. "Don Filippo, I'll do anything I could to right the wrong I did to Larry. I wanna come back home, to the neighborhood...but I want me an' my family to be safe."

"Do the right thing and you have my word…Larry's too."

"It's not just him. I got a bigger problem."

Googi, fingers drumming, looking around constantly, and wiping perspiration from his face, confesses to Don Filippo his part in framing Larry nine years earlier. He lays out how he got into trouble for distributing narcotics, which was a crime that called for a lengthy prison sentence from the law and a death sentence from the mob. He describes how pressure that was brought to bear on him from two different places led him to betray Larry and implicate him in crimes he had nothing to do with.

"…So, if I help Larry, an' tell what happened, youse gotta be able to protect me."

To their surprise, Johnny Brown and Sully enter the room through the back door that Googi had never locked.

"Protect you from what?"

Googi's eyes open wide with fear. He says, "No, Johnny…I didn't say nothing…I swear."

"On your life?"

Eyes bulging with fear, Googi goes silent.

"Why don't you get the fuck outta here, Johnny Brown, while you still could," Don Filippo says. "Larry's gonna be here any minute."

Johnny smiles as he pulls out a pistol with a silencer. "Is that so?"

* * * *

After slinking along the building line of the deserted street, Larry ducks into the back alley of Don Filippo's club. He looks all around at every shadow and every slice of light, watching for even the slightest movement in either, then quickly enters the club. When he steps into the club from the kitchen he makes out the forms of two men sitting at the table.

"Don Filippo?" he asks.

When he gets no answer, Larry slowly steps back to turn the light switch on. Don Filippo and Googi are both slumped at the table, blood running from their bodies into pools! Larry hurries to check Don Filippo for a sign of life; a breath, anything. Full of anguish at the cold breathless body, he hugs the old man's head before finally letting go of him. Images of the essential role the old man has played through his life as both a father figure and mob boss flash before him; the sound of his laughter, the feel of the face stubble when he kissed him in greeting or parting, the pride in his dark eyes when he'd inducted him into their family.

Larry shuts the light and leaves.

As he gets to the end of the alley and turns onto the street a police squad car pulls to a screeching halt. Two officers jump out of the car with guns drawn. One shines his flashlight directly into Larry's face. Larry takes off, running; his heart beating faster than his legs moving. One cop starts after him while the other calls on his two-way radio for assistance. The cop chasing Larry fires two shots that miss but blast chips off the brick wall that shower onto Larry's head and face just as he turns the corner.

When the cop rounds the corner, Larry has already disappeared into a warren of alleyways.

20

In a pre-dawn raid, SWAT Team members in bulletproof bests and helmets with face guards flood into the loft. They roughly manhandle J.C., Boom Boom, and Trickster as they roust, cuff, and take them away in police cars.

* * * *

On a television screen in Nicole's living room Mayor White is at the end of a press conference.

"...*You can rest assured that with yesterday's nomination,*" the Mayor says, "*I will now go on to win the Governorship and make sure that this city has enough funds to have its citizens go about their lives without the fear of violence. My recent record of reducing this city's random violence is only a sample of what we can and will do from Harrisburg.*"

Reporters call out questions over each other as the Mayor says, "*Thank you,*" and leaves, escorted by two bodyguards.

A photo inset of Larry appears on the screen, while the newscaster says, "*In other news, Philadelphia has had its first mob killing in quite a long time. Convicted mobster Larry Bellino, who was seen fleeing from the double murder of aging Mafia don, Filippo Alessi, and Arturo "Googi" Rosetti, was recently released from prison pending appeal of his ten year old narcotics conviction. Rosetti was the key witness in that case..."*

The television shuts off. Nicole, in a robe, appears weary; her eyes are red from crying. She holds a mug of coffee in one hand and tosses the remote control onto the sofa. Edward Marshall, hands clasped between his knees, sits at the edge of a club chair. "I'm sorry, but I told you it was only a matter of time until he murdered someone."

"I've got to get dressed," she says. "I have a wake to go to."

"You see now how right we were to get him off the streets."

"I don't want to talk about it."

Marshall hesitates then apprehensively asks, "I did not make the proverbial mistake we joke about, of allowing you to cover a mobster, did I?"

Nicole looks directly at him. Her expression is more weary than challenging. "Yes, Edward, you did. I *blew* the assignment. I also *fucked* the assignment. But then, Edward, we guineas are all cut from the same cloth anyway, aren't we?"

"Don't do this to yourself, Nicole...don't do this to us."

"There is no us, Edward," Nicole replies, "...and, to be perfectly truthful, there never was."

Edward Marshall sits there for a moment, his head hanging, then straightens up, stands, and without a word leaves.

* * * *

The morning of Don Filippo's funeral is bathed in sunlight that contrasts with the dark sadness of the large crowd of mourners who stand around the coffin. The final words come from the priest, Father Vincent, who happens to be Don Filippo and Mimi's son. Their daughter, Theresa, a nun, stands on one side of Mimi; Nicole stands on the other. All of the others in attendance are old people; the preponderance of them men from the club. On the other side of the nun, is Anna, Don Filippo's older sister.

"...And so, with love," Father Vincent says, "we commit to earth the body of a dear father, husband, brother, and friend, Filippo Vincenzo Giovanni Alessi, and leave to You, Oh Lord, his Soul. Amen."

Suddenly, Anna steps forward and screams, "No! Noooo!! Don't go! Filippo, my baby brother, we love you! Noooo!"

While the nun and the OLD PERSON on the other side of Anna hold her arms to keep her from throwing herself onto the coffin, Mimi steps to her and grabs her shoulder hard. "Anna, your brother always hated when you did that shit at funerals," she says matter-of-factly. "If you don't shut up he's gonna come back and haunt you...and I'm gonna break your fuckin' face."

Nicole, whose own family suffers their individual and group sorrow in silence, is taken aback by the scene. She entwines her arm with Mimi's and walks her back to the hearse. Father Vincent and Sister Theresa follow, calming their Aunt Anna as they walk.

When Nicole and Mimi get into the hearse, they are surprised to see Larry sitting in the back seat. He is unshaven and looks extremely worn out by recent events. Nicole throws herself into his arms. Mimi sits on the other side of him and kisses him too.

"*Oopatzo!*" Mimi says. "You know what a chance you took, coming here?"

"How could I stay away?"

Mimi's son, daughter, and sister-in-law Anna pile in. All are confused, as they have never met the disheveled person they see Mimi and Nicole hugging. Mimi introduces Larry as being like a second son to her and Don Filippo. They greet him cautiously, obviously having seen his photo on news reports. The chauffeur silently begins to drive.

"You know about the boys?" Mimi asks.

"I heard. Mimi, you know I got nothing to do –"

"Don't say another word," Mimi snaps, "or I'll beat you on the head myself. Filippo loved you...an' I know…" When she begins to get teary, she waves her hand dismissingly. "I don't wanna talk about it no more."

Nicole asks Larry, "Where have you been staying?"

"Around."

Nicole reaches into her bag. "Here, take this key to my place: 950 West 56th Street, apartment 8B, on the top floor. No one will look for you there."

"No. I don't want to jeopardize you."

"Nothing scares us guineas," she says and kisses him again.

"You're supposed to pick up the good habits," he tells her. "Whoever whacked Googi and the old man, and I could only think of one guy it could be, is gonna be looking for me next." At that moment, the car passes the funeral for Rachel. In contrast, most of the mourners are young.

Larry calls to the chauffeur, "Yo, pull over here for a minute."

When they stop, Larry rolls down one of the tinted windows. He just stares out until Pepe looks over toward him. Their eyes meet in shared agony.

* * * *

Soon after, everyone except Larry gathers at Don Filippo's club. The entire place has been turned into a makeshift catering hall for the post-funeral meal. Mismatched tables and chairs are crowded together. None of the tableware matches either. Food, however, is plentiful, in chafing dishes set up in the rear; its smell of garlic, onions, and tomatoes permeate the club with sweetness. The crowd is made up of mourners from both Don Filippo's and Rachel's funerals. Funzi approaches Pepe, who stands off by himself, not eating. "Come'ere," he says, and leads Pepe to a closet that holds electronic equipment, including the suitcase of dials used to detect listening devices. He goes on, "I don't think we're gonna need any of this stuff anymore. You youngsters'll make better use of it..." Funzi stops talking when he notices an empty spot where a piece of equipment had been.

At that moment a pay phone in the club rings. One of the old men who are always around the club, answers it then lets it hang while he goes to Nicole. "Phone, for you," he tells her.

Nicole goes to take it, excited that it may be from Larry. "Hello?"

On the other end a man's gravelly voice asks, "Yeah, Miss Gianetti?"

"Yes?"

"I'm calling for Larry. He sez he wants you to meet him."

Nicole, surprised and wary, asks, "Where is he?"

"I'll tell you where to go; then somebody'll pick you up an' take you to him," the man answers. "Just make sure you come alone."

"Tell me, what is he wearing?" she asks.

"What is this, the third degree?" the voice says. "You either want to see him, or you don't."

When Nicole remains silent, the phone clicks off. Nicole dials the phone to her apartment, but only gets a constant unanswered ring.

* * * *

Larry watches the phone ring in Nicole's apartment. He is tempted to answer, but resists. He's made sure GPS can't track him by dumping his mobile phone and won't take a stupid chance now.

* * * *

The phone in Nicole's apartment continues to ring without an answer on her third try. "Shit!" she says and hangs up the phone receiver. She hurries over to the chauffeur, who has his face buried in an eggplant *parmigiano* hero. "Please, you have to drive me somewhere...immediately. I have to warn Larry." Nicole goes to Mimi, whispers in her ear, then grabs her bag and hurries out with the chauffeur.

No sooner does Nicole leave than Funzi, who is still with Pepe trying to figure out what happened to the missing equipment, gets an idea. "Oh shit! I'll bet I know where it is." Funzi rushes to the table where the don used to sit and orders Pepe to crawl underneath it. Pepe finds a small tape recorder hooked into a makeshift holder beneath the table. He removes it then hands it to Funzi and shimmies back out. Pepe takes a beefy hand offered by Funzi to help get him stand, though his youth allows him to do it on his own. The old man tries to play the recorder, but it doesn't work.

"*Ma vancoulo*," Funzi curses, "the battery's dead." He tells Pepe, "C'mon."

With Pepe following, Funzi quickly carries the recorder into the club's kitchen. He takes new batteries from a drawer, replaces them in the machine, rewinds the tape then pushes the play button. They hear Googi's voice, "*Thank you, Don Filippo, for leaving the door open. I wouldn't want to wait outside an extra minute, even at this time of night.*"

Don Filippo's voice follows, "*Whose fault is that?*"

They play the tape; everyone in the club has crowded around the recorder. They listen intently, and sadly, to each word.

Near the end of the tape they hear Don Filippo say, "*Why don't you get the fuck outta here, Johnny Brown, while you still could. Larry's gonna be here any minute.*"

"*Is that so?*" Johnny Brown replies on the tape, instantly followed by the popping sounds of silencer-muffled gunfire and screams of Googi. Gasps from the crowd mingle with the sanguinary sounds of Googi being murdered.

Then comes the voice of Don Filippo, *"Rot in Hell, you sonomabitch!"* followed by more silencer gunfire. The gasps of the crowd become cries of anguish and curses in Italian and English directed at Johnny Brown. Tears run down Mimi's face. She suddenly realizes Nicole is not there.

"Nicole," she says. "Oh shit! Pepe, come here!"

* * * *

Johnny, Sully, and Carmine follow behind the limo taking Nicole to her home and Larry. Johnny Brown is filled with bloody anticipation of killing Larry and the fun he intends to have with Nicole before disposing of her too. He thinks that he may enjoy having Larry watch while he has his way with her. The thoughts make his head pound and an erection form.

* * * *

In Nicole's apartment at the same time Larry is out of the shower, in his shorts, looking at the photo of Nicole's parents, in Florida. Soon he hears a key being inserted into the front door. Smiling, he hurries behind the door to surprise Nicole when she enters. Instead of Nicole, however, it is Edward Marshall who comes in, carrying a bouquet of flowers. Shocked, Larry slams the door shut behind Marshall.

"Oh, my God –" Marshall blurts out.

Larry hits Marshall on the jaw, sending him reeling backwards and down onto the floor. Marshall raises himself on an elbow, shakes his head to try to clear it, then hangs it back and groans. He is as much emotionally deflated, from seeing Larry in his underwear at Nicole's place, as he is physically dizzied by the punch.

"What the fuck are you doing here?" Larry asks.

"What do you think, genius? Key...flowers..."

"You and Nicole?"

"Who ever said gangsters were dumb?"

Larry is both stunned and hurt at the same time. "Get up, you fuckin' hardon," he says.

Marshall continues to lie there; head back and eyes closed. "For you to hit me again? Sorry."

"I said, get up."

"Do whatever you want," the D.A. says. "It is all over anyway...everything."

Larry steps over and drags Edward Marshall, who offers no resistance or defense, up to face him. Marshall has no spirit left, and diverts his eyes from Larry's.

"I should kill you."

* * * *

Downstairs, Nicole's limo makes a sharp stop in front of the building. She immediately jumps out and hurries into the building. Carmine's car pulls up in back of the limo. Johnny Brown and Sully get out; Carmine swings the car into a good getaway spot across the street, where he can watch them from. As the two men rush after Nicole, Sully stops by the parked limo, opens the driver's side door and fires a bullet into the chauffeur's head from a silencer-equipped pistol, then follows Johnny into the building.

Johnny and Sully catch Nicole at the elevator, just as it is about to open. She instantly recognizes the danger, but it is too late. Johnny shoves her, screaming for help, into the elevator, where she crashes into a young man about to leave.

"Hey, what's going on?" the young man asks, seconds before Sully pumps two silencer-bullets into his chest.

"Oh no! God!" Nicole cries out.

Johnny grabs Nicole and sticks a pistol under her chin as the elevator door closes. "Just shut the fuck up and do what I tell you," he says.

* * * *

Just as Larry shoves Ed Marshall backwards onto a sofa, the apartment door swings open and Nicole stumbles in ahead of Johnny Brown and Sully. She falls forward and lands on the floor from Johnny's push. Larry, who, though shocked, starts toward her, stops when he sees the guns pointed at him. Ed Marshall sits up on the sofa.

"Hey, hey, the gang's all here," Johnny says.

Marshall says, "What the hell?!"

Johnny Brown turns toward Ed Marshall and nods in recognition. "Mr. District Attorney."

"Favara," the D.A. says, "do you know what you are doing?!"

"Somebody's gotta clean up your mess."

"Have you lost your mind?"

"You know, I'm really disappointed in you," Johnny Brown says to Ed Marshall. "I handed you this guy on a silver platter nine years ago, and now you let him slip off."

Nicole looks at Larry, understanding now that he was really framed. Guilt for not fully believing him overwhelms all the other emotions swirling within her. Larry, however, glares at her, pissed off that she's been dating Marshall.

The D.A. says to Johnny Brown, "You gave me a witness to save yourself. I did my job...that's it."

"C'mon, counselor, you know better than that. You knew that Googi was a fuckin' liar."

"No...I...I..."

Johnny Brown continues, "You looked the other way so you could go after the bigger dick." He smiles sardonically at Larry. "...Though I'm not so sure that last part's true...the bigger dick part."

While Johnny directs his conversation with Larry, Nicole and Ed Marshall conduct their own, creating a cacophony of simultaneous arguing.

"Edward...how could you?" Nicole implores angrily.

Johnny taunts Larry, "Maybe we'll let your girlfriend decide after she tries mine? Maybe Sully's too?"

Marshall defends himself to Nicole, "Don't look at me like that. I made a choice, in the public's interest."

"Don't even think about it," Larry says to Johnny Brown.

Nicole asks Ed Marshall, "When did you become God?"

Larry glowers at Johnny Brown. The two men's eyes are locked in a challenge, like two jungle animals. Johnny's eyes dare Larry to make a move. The only thing keeping Larry from pouncing on Johnny Brown's throat is the gun Johnny is pointing at him.

"Nicole, be reasonable," Ed Marshall says. "We do it all the time...every time we make a deal. It's a compromise...a choice."

Satisfied that he's got the upper hand, Johnny Brown turns his attention to Ed Marshall and Nicole. "Hey, D.A., relax; don't get your balls in an uproar. What you did then was okay. It's your sloppy handling now that's the problem. I even had to glom the old file out of your office or you woulda left it there for this douchebag to find."

"Hey, wait a minute!" Ed snaps. "Who do you think you're
_"

Johnny Brown swings his pistol around to point at Ed Marshall, and cocks it while Nicole's fingers worm their way unnoticed into her pocketbook.

"Don't be a fuckin' hero!" Johnny tells Ed Marshall. "Now

is your last chance to save yourself and walk out of here, alive and with a good friend in the streets. Otherwise, you die with them."

* * * *

Outside, at the same time as the ruckus continues in Nicole's apartment, a car pulls up with Pepe, Mimi, and two of Pepe's friends. They all get out, leaving the car double-parked and stopped next to the limo Nicole arrived in. Pepe opens the passenger-side door to see the limo driver dead. They gasp at the bloody corpse then head for the building.

"Wait here!" Pepe tells Mimi. "If you could, call the cops!"

Mimi yells after him, "I don't call fuckin' cops!"

* * * *

From his car parked across the street, Carmine watches Pepe and his group rush into Nicole's building.

* * * *

Pepe and his friends get off the second elevator at the eighth floor. They look into the other elevator, which Johnny Brown has stopped on that floor, and see the dead man.

Sonny Girard

* * * *

Outside, Carmine has come across the street to collar Mimi. He drags her into the lobby and toward the elevator at gunpoint.

"Don't make me kill you, grandma," he tells her.

"Fuck you, you sonomabitch bastard!" She too fumbles in her bag as they wait for the one operating elevator to arrive. A young couple with a baby in a carriage also comes toward the elevator.

Carmine tells Mimi in a low voice, "Shut up or I'll kill you an' them too."

* * * *

Outside the building a police patrol car with two cops pulls up by the double-parked car, as a few people have been looking into the limo. A woman runs to the police car, screaming about the murder. One of the officers gets on the phone for backup, while his partner, gun drawn, runs into the building. The officer with the gun reaches the lobby just as the couple with a child is about to enter the elevator. Carmine holds Mimi at gunpoint, ready to follow them in.

The officer yells, "Everyone, stay where you are!"

Carmine lets go of Mimi as he turns and fires at the officer, hitting him. Mimi gets into the elevator. The doors are about

138

closed when Carmine manages to get his foot in and pry them open. Mimi squirts lighter fluid through the flame of her cigarette lighter onto Carmine's chest. He jumps back, trying to put out the flames spreading upward on his shirt as the doors close. He fires his pistol repeatedly at the closing doors.

* * * *

Upstairs, Pepe's friends hug the wall on either side of Nicole's apartment door. Pepe makes the sign of the cross over his chest then lifts a fist to bang on the door. "Larry, it's me!" he shouts then steps to the side wall.

Sully turns and fires through the center of the door.

Pepe steps further out of the way just as the bullets splinter the door where he had previously stood.

Larry takes the opportunity of Sully's firing at the door to jump him and grab his gun hand. When Johnny Brown swings his pistol toward Larry and Sully, Nicole draws the pepper spray from her bag and aims it in Johnny's direction. He turns in time to see it coming and ducks out of the way, then aims the pistol at Nicole. Ed Marshall jumps on Johnny Brown and smothers him in a bear hug as Johnny gets off three shots. All of whose bullets explode through Ed Marshall's body.

Nicole screams and drops both her bag and the pepper spray.

At that moment, the sound of police sirens draws everyone's attention. Pepe's kicking on the door makes it creak and shimmy, signaling it won't take long to open. Johnny Brown grabs Nicole by her hair and drags her toward the window. He opens it and pulls her out onto and up the fire-escape to the roof.

Larry, who has been fighting with Sully, has managed to get him to drop the gun, but is getting the worst of their hand to hand combat. The door bursts open and Pepe and his friends rush through. They immediately jump Sully to help Larry who backs away for a breath. He tries to get the gun, but the four men struggling are between him and it on the floor near the doorway. Larry leaves the gun and, instead, heads out the window after Johnny Brown and Nicole.

In spite of being outnumbered, Sully manages to beat the shit out of Pepe and his friends when the elevator opens and Mimi rushes out. She sees the scene, spots the gun on the floor, picks it up, and when Sully is in the clear shoots him in the chest.

"Give me that," Pepe says. He takes the gun from Mimi then takes off out the window after Larry, Johnny, and Nicole.

* * * *

On the roof, Johnny Brown, still drags Nicole along with him by her hair. He fires two shots at Larry, who follows them from their left side. Johnny backs into the corner of the roof, where the protective wall is about waist high in back of him and Nicole. Larry stops behind a small shed-like structure.

"You shoulda stayed in jail, Larry," Johnny yells. "You fucked up the program, now you gotta pay the piper. Come on out."

"Let her go, Johnny, an' I'll come out."

Johnny Brown laughs. "I look like a fuckin' moron to you?" he says. "You got till I count three, then the cunt goes over the side with an air-conditioned skull. One..."

"Let her go, Johnny!"

"Two..."

Suddenly, Pepe comes onto the roof and runs around to Johnny's right side. When he spots Johnny, he points the gun at him."

"Let her go!"

Johnny reels around and, letting go of Nicole who drops to the ground and scurries away on her hands and knees, shoots at Pepe. A bullet hits Pepe, sending him spinning backwards and onto the ground.

Larry, who has taken off on the run since the moment Johnny began to turn toward Pepe, charges him. Johnny turns the gun on Larry and fires, but is out of ammunition. Larry hasn't missed a step. He tackles Johnny, smashing him against the roof's protective half-wall. They fall to the ground fighting, and manage to get up again. The battle is brutal, with punches that would break bones and on anyone less fit. Both men use every trick they learned as kids brawling in the streets among themselves and with those from nearby neighborhoods; they use grips on each other's heads to smash them on the floor or against the wall; they kick and bite as if they were Mike Tyson going at Evander Holyfield's ear. Both want to kill. Johnny doesn't care how, just as long as he gets rid of Larry, who's been a thorn in his side since they were kids. Larry wants to feel the last pulse of Johnny's life fade. Killing him isn't enough; shooting isn't enough. The rage of his lost years and the old man's death fill him with a lust to drain the life from Johnny or have a stroke from the hate that fills every cell of his body.

Johnny finally seems to gain an edge. He has Larry against the wall, pushing him backwards, dangerously close toward what could be a fall to his death, when another shot rings out. It chips the wall next to the two fighting men. Johnny takes a half-step back for a moment. Larry sees it is Nicole with the smoking pistol, the one that Pepe had dropped when he was shot.

"For Christ's sake," Larry shouts, "move in close! Shoot him!"

Frightened half to death, Nicole moves in closer. Johnny Brown continues to pin Larry down as their struggle continues. A second shot makes Johnny jerk up, as he is winged on his arm. "Shit!" he snaps.

Larry orders Nicole, "Closer! Shoot him!"

Nicole inches closer. The men reverse positions a couple of times, making it difficult for her to fire. Johnny Brown hits Larry with a punch that rocks him. Nicole moves next to them with the pistol aimed with two hands. Johnny, who is on top, swings Larry around between him and Nicole just as she fires again -- but it only clicks as empty as Johnny's did.

Larry stops for a split-second, shocked -- enough time for Johnny to swing him around over the wall again. Johnny grabs Nicole's wrist and pulls her into the fracas. Now Larry is more cautious as he tries to struggle out from underneath without having Nicole thrown over the side. "Let her go, you fuck!" Larry says. "Nicole, bite him! Run!"

Nicole pounds Johnny Brown's head with the gun in her free hand until he releases his hold on her.

"Fuckin' bitch!"

Larry seizes the moment to swing out from underneath Johnny Brown, so that their positions have reversed. A police officer charges up to the roof's doorway with a gun pointed at Nicole. She steps over to blocks clear view of Larry, who now has Johnny hanging over the side of the roof.

"Drop the gun!" the officer shouts.

"I'm an assistant district attorney."

"I don't care who you are. Drop the gun!"

Nicole stares at the cop for a moment, as though undecided about what to do, then lets the gun slip out of her hand and drop to the ground.

Johnny Brown glares up at Larry. Confident that he is now safe with a cop on the roof he stops his struggle and allows Larry to hold him like a rag doll. Johnny smiles as if to say, *I beat you again, jerkoff.* Larry turns his head to look in the direction of the officer, breathes deeply, starts to lift Johnny up…then, thinking *fuck feeling him die,* raises his hands high in the air and turns around, letting Johnny Brown fall over the side of the roof and to his death.

21

A couple of months later, toward mid-November, Larry's immediate neighborhood is revitalized. Green, white, and red garland decorations full of tiny glittery lights span above traffic from one side of the street to the other, giving the area a festival look. Stores display Thanksgiving decorations in their windows. J.C.'s Deli sports an LED sign that reads *"ONLY 12 DAYS TO GET THE BIRD."* A number of people walk along the streets. A few stores are open and doing business, including the barbershop, though the area appears to be one that is busy in the daytime but still has a way to go before it can be secure enough to be considered a night time hub too.

The store that housed Don Filippo's club has a new front and a sign announcing, *DON FILIPPO'S -- RISTORANTE ITALIANO.* A warm inviting glow emanates from inside.

Inside, the busy but not completely full restaurant is decorated in an old Southern Italian style that has disappeared from the restaurant scene years before: red tablecloths, paintings of the Sicilian coastline and Palermo's fresh food markets, crystal sconces. It appears to be a family-type eatery nostalgic for its roots. On one wall a portrait of Don Filippo hangs proudly; a crucifix on purple bunting decorates the bottom of the frame.

The crowd of diners, though not having the appearance of neighborhood residents, seems to especially enjoy the revitalized area and warmth of the restaurant. One group of patrons, led by Larry's crew, indulge themselves by singing "Santa Lucia" at the top of their untrained voices. One might think them half-drunk if not for the fact that there are no drinks other than sparkling water on the tables.

On a rear wall a sign pronounces, *"Congratulations Governor White."* The words *Congratulations* and *Governor* are hand-written above the crossed out *Elect* and *Mayor*. Governor-elect White stands near the sign along with Nicole and Larry, who stand as close to each other as Siamese Twins. Nicole's gently swelling abdomen announces the first trimester of pregnancy.

"You know, Ed Marshall would have loved to see the results of his efforts," the Mayor-turned-Governor says. "Too bad."

"Yes, I am sure he would have," Nicole agrees.

Governor-elect White goes on, "You know, our D.A. was one of the few people I have ever known who was always more concerned about this city than himself."

"A true hero," Larry says, trying not to overdo the sarcasm he intends.

Nicole gets his meaning and out of Jonathon White's view pinches his ass as punishment.

White ignores Larry's remark addresses Nicole again, "He would not have been happy, however, to see us losing you on the job. We will...I will miss you."

"I think my husband needs me more, to help him with his restaurant," she replies, then pats her swollen stomach with unusually moist palms. "Not to mention his other needs. He's like the bunny with the battery...day and night."

Larry's face flushes with embarrassment. "You're

definitely hanging out with Mimi too much," he says. To Nicole, Mimi Alessi has given her the nurturing and warmth that she never had from her own mother after her earliest years, and she's found herself picking up so many of the old lady's traits; behavior she would have frowned on for most of her life. Most of all, Mimi has taught her to embrace her heritage, which has liberated her to expose an abundance of affection that had stayed buried in her for too long.

The former Mayor laughs at Nicole's remark about Larry's sexual appetite. "You can't blame the man," he says. "After nine years, what do you expect?"

Nicole replies, "That was not a complaint."

A man and woman enter. They stop and speak to a waiter then walk back to Larry and Nicole. "Table for two?"

"Sorry," Nicole says, "but we're all booked for tonight."

The man and woman look around at the empty seats. The woman asks, "If we wait, will there be something?"

"Not tonight," Nicole answers with a smile. "But I can take a reservation for any other time."

As the annoyed couple leaves, Larry shrugs to Jonathon White, who gives him a look of understanding. Larry tells him, "Go ahead, sit down and enjoy. The *pasta fazoole* should be coming out any second now."

"Yes, please," Nicole adds. "I ordered some special Cristal Rose for a toast." She curses under her breath that she can't drink because of her pregnancy. *If anyone ever needed a drink*, she thinks, *it's me.*

"What do you want to do, get us locked up, here?" Larry

asks. "We ain't got our liquor license yet."

Governor-elect White responds, "Don't worry, you've got a friend in high places." He adds, "Give me a call tomorrow and I will personally have it taken care of posthaste."

"The faces are different," Larry says, "but something feels very familiar about that."

They all laugh. Larry and Nicole escort Jonathon White to a long table with about two dozen guests, including J.C., Trickster, Boom Boom, a few politician and police types, Mimi, Funzi, Pepe, and Pepe's two friends, who were involved in the fiasco at Nicole's building. Larry's men have just finished singing *"Santa Lucia."* J.C. and Trickster begin singing *"Hey, Compare,"* alone while everyone else claps their hands and stamps their feet.

* * * *

While the celebratory atmosphere continues inside the restaurant, a car pulls to the curb outside. Two men in long coats get out of the car and walk toward the restaurant.

* * * *

Inside, the cheerful atmosphere with the singing of *"Hey, Compare"* continues. All the guests seem to be having the time of their lives. Larry stands with his arm around Nicole. She tightly clutches the back of his suit jacket.

Suddenly the door swings open and Carmine stands in the doorway. He lifts a machine gun from under his coat. A second man stands behind and to the side of him to protect his rear. Carmine's face is flush with anger.

Larry pulls Nicole down to the floor behind the table that has been thrown on its side as gunfire erupts. He shields her with his body between her and the table in case any bullets happen to get through the reinforcements he had installed. He cups her ears in both his hands to protect them from the explosive blasts.

A deadly silence follows the end of shooting. Everyone who has hit the floor behind the table where the party was in progress remains still. Though it might appear that everyone is dead, there are no bullet holes in the overturned reinforced table or blood on those on the ground. Everyone else in the restaurant is also on the floor, except the front tables nearest the door, where four detectives stand with smoking shotguns in their hands. They had been expecting Carmine, and have ambushed him; his and his accomplice's shredded and bloody forms cover an area larger than their living size. The shotguns have also blown out a good portion of the restaurant's front door and windows. Blood, body bits, glass, and splinters of wood reach onto parked cars. Carmine's getaway car and driver have gotten away.

As the other patrons rise, they all pull badges and hook them on their outer clothing. They have pistols drawn and, after seeing that the danger is over and their co-workers have won, go about their business of taking care of the crime scene -- roping off the outside, digging out and bagging spent bullets from Carmine's gun; all the routine CSI investigative work. There is not much difference between the scene at *Don Filippo's Ristorante* and the *Pinar del Rio Restaurant*, where a young child's birthday party slaughter prompted then Mayor Jonathon White to put into action alternative measures to quell crime in his city.

Larry is the first to rise at the large rear table. He pulls Nicole up and extends a hand to Governor-elect White. Slowly, everyone else gets up. Hesitant at first, they become joyful to see it is over and they are still alive.

"You okay?" Larry asks Nicole.

Still shaken up, she only nods as he pulls her close.

"Well, you were right," Jonathon White says. "Putting out word of a party did draw him out. It took balls, but we will all sleep better now."

"For a night or two, anyway," Larry replies. "But, I gotta admit, the one with balls is really you. I was raised to take life and death chances…you weren't."

The new Governor tells Larry that he underestimates the commitment of average law-abiding Americans to fight when necessary; that the detectives who provided the buffer for them while risking their own lives are the same kind of people who won world wars for the country and brought down a plane over Pennsylvania on 9/11 to save others in Washington, D.C. He lightens up when he talks about Larry's contribution, "We all owe you a tremendous debt," he says. "I think I just might have to make you Police Commissioner."

"Thanks, but no thanks," Larry responds. "My father and grandfather would come back from the dead to kill me." He adds, "A new storefront and paying for the other damage will be enough."

"You know how anemic our budget is. It will probably have to wait until I get to Harrisburg."

Larry shrugs. "It figures."

By that time, everyone at their large main table is back in his or her seat. J.C. is the first to break their silence, "Whoa, what is this, a wake or a celebration?"

"Yeah," Trickster chimes in, "where were we?"

J.C. says, "Take it from the top," they begin singing "*Hey, Compare*" again.

Nicole observes her image in a bullet-shattered mirror at the rear service bar. The woman she sees is one she would never have recognized as anyone related to her, but one related to a larger cultural community: dark, Mediterranean hair, makeup that accentuates the exotic almond shape of her eyes, a blouse that dips to reveal the swelling breasts of approaching motherhood. She smiles at the fact that the reflection is also someone confident and tough enough to withstand incidents like this that have plagued her ancestors for centuries...and someone who looks comfortable in her own skin and content...even more: happy.

She says to Larry, "I hope this is the end of your past life, Mr. Bellino."

"I don't know, Mrs. Bellino," he replies. "To tell the truth, I felt a lot safer as a crook."

"It's not about you or me anymore." Nicole pats her stomach. "I think there's going to be a whole lot of little Bellinos we'll have to worry about first." She hugs and kisses Larry. "Come upstairs with me," she says. "I want to show you how we Italians really make pasta fazoole to spice up your life."

Larry walks off with an arm around her. "An' you go telling me it's the rabbit in the family," he says. "What a con artist you are."

"You love it."

"You bet," he says and plants another kiss on her. "Pasta fazoole…that's a good one."

"That's what you get when you marry an Italian girl."

La Fine (The End)

COMING SOON: ALL NEW!

25 ORIGINAL ORGANIZED CRIME CROSS-WORD PUZZLES BY FORMER-MOBSTER-TURNED-AUTHOR SONNY GIRARD.

To contact Sonny Girard with comments or questions, or to order autographed copies of any of his books go to www.SonnysMobCafe.com. It is the <u>only</u> place signed copies are available.

Also by Sonny Girard:

Sonny Girard's Mob Reader

Sonny Girard's Mob Reader is the ultimate organized crime primer from someone who's actually spent his entire life as an insider and writes without confessions. Unlike mob turncoats (i.e.: rats) he writes authentically without self-serving, gratuitous excuses. His old friends, whoever's left, are still his best friends. Mob Reader contains his original articles, short snapshots of mostly unknown characters, reviews of his favorite mob books, letters from visitors to www.SonnysMobCafe.com, and sample pages of his previously published novels.

"SEX AND ROMANCE, MOBSTERS AND SPIES. WHAT MORE COULD A GIRL ASK FOR?"

- Kim Delaney, actor, "NYPD Blue" (ABC-TV)

"Mob Reader captures the heart of the mob life without glorifying it or attacking it; just tells it like it is."

- Jennifer Graziano, Creator and Executive Producer of "Mob Wives" franchise, VH-1

"Sonny Girard's Mob Reader takes you on a journey into the real mob: how they killed, intriguing, suspenseful, with an insider's view of life in the mob"

- Tony "Nap" Napoli, best selling author of *My Father My Don*

"Nobody knows the inside outs of mob life better than Sonny. No bullshit; no lies. Sonny Girard's Mob Reader is great reading."

- Frank DiMatteo, Publisher, Mob Candy Magazine

Also by Sonny Girard:

BLOOD OF OUR FATHERS

"An authentic thriller from a mob guy who's obviously been there."

-- **Nicholas Pileggi, Author of** *Wiseguy (Film name: Goodfellas)*

With razor-sharp honesty, Sonny Girard, an ex-mobster himself, tells the story of "Mickey Boy" Messina, just paroled from prison for a crime he didn't commit, and in love with his brother's ex-girlfriend, Laurel, a complication on his road to becoming a "made man" in the Calabra Crime Family. Mickey Boy's mother, Connie, carries a secret of an affair that could cost her son his life. Chrissy Augusta, a top mobster's teenage daughter, walks a dangerous tightrope with a secret lover from another *Cosa Nostra* family. All three affairs collide with tragic results in the midst of a bloody mob war.

From Little Italy social clubs to mob bedrooms, BLOOD OF OUR FATHERS is a tale of intimacy, loyalty and betrayal in the underworld – an underworld caught up in a war that threatens the life of everyone associated with it. Three love stories in a mob setting rather than a mob story, BLOOD OF OUR FATHER portrays family secrets, authentic organized crime politics, and bloodshed that crackles with vivid detail.

"Girard shines as a storyteller...(he has an) authoritative grasp of the Mafia's inner workings."

-- *Publishers Weekly*

"This story is not just for guys. It's like Jackie Collins meets Mario Puzo. I loved it."

--*Katherine Narducci, Actor (Sopranos, Bronx Tale, etc.)*

"Sonny Girard captures the heart of the mob life without glorifying it or attacking it; just tells it like it is."

- **Jennifer Graziano, Creator and Executive Producer of "Mob Wives" franchise, VH-1**

Also by Sonny Girard:

SINS OF OUR SONS

Not since Mario Puzo's **Godfather** *has a novel so passionately captured the soul of organized crime as did mob insider Sonny Girard's astounding debut,* **Blood of Our Fathers.** *Now Girard brings us the extraordinary successor, an explosive drama of the changes rocking the American Mafia...*

In one swift stroke, an assassin's bullet elevated Mickey Boy Messina from foot soldier to boss of the Calabra Crime Family – and left him with a legacy of pain and confusion. Now Mickey Boy is walking a delicate line, caught between the thrill of a power he never dreamed would be his, and Frank Halloran, a rock-hard parole officer determined to bring him down; between Don Peppino Palermo, a treacherous old Sicilian boss scheming to change the face of New York's organized crime, and Laurel, Mickey Boy's smart, sexy, no-nonsense wife. For her sake – and for the sake of Hope, the baby daughter he prayed for to end his line of mob inheritance – Mickey Boy is filled with a new ambition: to lead his people away from their criminal tradition and into the legitimate world. But in a dark society laced with misplaced trusts, and peppered with sudden and violent revenge, the road into daylight has always been paved with blood and sorrow...

"Sonny Girard...takes you on a journey into the real mob: how they killed, intriguing, suspenseful, with an insider's view of life in the mob"

-    Tony "Nap" Napoli, author of "My Father, My Don"

"Nobody knows the inside outs of mob life better than Sonny. No bullshit; no lies."

- Frank DiMatteo, Publisher, Mob Candy Magazine

[Sonny Girard is] "*...A man who knows the world of crime.*"

-- **Bill O'Reilly,** *The O'Reilly Factor,* **Fox News Channel**

155

Also by Sonny Girard:

SNAKE EYES

Small-time mobster Neil DiChristo is a happy-go-lucky bookmaker who prefers wine, women, and good food, not necessarily in that order, to any serious work or crime. One morning he is dragged out of his house by a team of FBI agents who have put together enough false information to throw him in prison for life and mark him as an informant to get him killed. All they want, they say, is for him to get close enough to a Russian operative to bring him down. It seems the only chink is the Russian's gambling habit, and DiChristo's credentials in that area give him the greatest chance of gaining the supposed spy's confidence. With no good option available, he reluctantly agrees.

From the opening page, Neil DiChristo is catapulted into a bizarre world of intrigue, murder, and more sex and romance than is healthy for anyone—where nothing is as it seems and his fate is beyond his control. All Neil wants is to be left alone.

Fat chance.

"Girard shines as a storyteller."

—Publisher's Weekly

"Sex and romance, mobsters and spies. What more could a girl ask for?"

—Kim Delaney, Actor (*NYPD Blue* – ABC TV).

"Sonny certainly knows all the players, and when it comes to this kind of book he's as good as anyone."

—James Caan, Actor (*Godfather, Vegas*/NBC-TV, *etc.*)

"Girard captivates the reader. He is an accomplished storyteller."

—Literary Journal

ABOUT THE AUTHOR

Sonny Girard was born on the Lower East Side of Manhattan but raised but raised in the Red Hook and Navy Yard sections of Brooklyn: Mob Country. He has spent the greater part of his adult life on the inside of organized crime, not as a hanger-on or sycophant, but as a full time participant.

The target of a three-and-a-half year undercover investigation by New York's Organized Crime Control Bureau. Sonny was characterized by the New York Post as a "...middle echelon member"of one of New York's five mob families. His arrest resulted in a three year sentence in State Prison, where he maxed out in facilities like Sing Sing, Dannemora, Downstate, and Arthurkill.

Convicted later of racketeering under the R.I.C.O. Organized Crime Statute by Rudy Giuliani's office, and sentenced to seven years in Federal Prison, Sonny Girard again served the maximum time allowed under the law. It was during that time that he wrote the first of his three novels, "Blood of Our Fathers," which was published by Pocket/Simon & Schuster.